Reg.

$\dfrac{0}{11-18}$

Np

FIC   Rhode, Robert, 1911-

        Sandstone

DATE			

SANDSTONE

Robert Rhode

WALKER AND COMPANY
NEW YORK

First published in the United States of America in 1982
by the Walker Publishing Company, Inc.

Published simultaneously in Canada by John Wiley &
Sons Canada, Limited, Rexdale, Ontario.

ISBN: 0-8027-4015-4

Library of Congress Catalog Card Number:
    82-60150

Printed in the United States of America

10 9 8 7 6 5 4 3 2 1

Dedicated to Mary and Carman Rhode, who taught me how to tell the good guys from the bad.

CHAPTER 1

BY the fourth bong of the bank's grandfather clock, Elizabeth Castle was desperate enough to try anything. She heard the last of the bank customers being ushered out and she heard the door lock click into place. Someone was lowering the window shades. She tried to control her shaking hand as she lifted the derringer out of her purse and pointed it at the chest of Alfred Pound, president of Tucson Cattlemen's Bank.

"I want fifty thousand dollars placed on this desk," she said politely, "and I want it before that clock reads one minute past four."

Pound stared hard with disbelieving eyes and didn't move. "You have forty-five seconds left, Mr. Pound."

He rose stiffly and hesitated, as if weighing his chances, then walked quickly to the door. He opened it about halfway and spoke softly to a clerk seated just outside. "Miss Ruther, please have Mr. Stringfellow bring me fifty thousand dollars. Quickly, Miss Ruther."

The tall, portly man turned back to Elizabeth. His puffy face was flushed with anger. "You're a foolish woman, Miss Castle. That money's mine and I intend to get it back." He spit out each word. "You will pay for this indecency."

The conviction in his voice sent a shiver down her back. She resisted the urge to run for the door. She must not allow herself to panic. She had to think about details.

"I'll need something to carry the money in, something that will disguise it," she said.

Pound sneered and fingered his gold watch fob. "You are the clever thief, aren't you, Miss Castle?" He didn't take his eyes off her. "Miss Ruther!" he shouted through the open doorway.

A petite, middle-aged woman appeared with a teller's tray filled with bundles of bills. She froze when she saw Elizabeth's gun.

"Miss Ruther," Pound said, "now find a sack to put it in. There, beside your desk, that will do."

"But . . . but . . . Mr. Pound, that's the bag for my knitting . . . for my needles and yarn and . . ."

"Bring it, Miss Ruther," Pound said sternly.

Elizabeth hated to take the woman's bag, but it would be dangerous to show feelings of sympathy. The woman brought in a white cotton sack decorated with embroidery. A red ribbon was attached neatly to the top for drawing the sack closed. As Pound and Miss Ruther stuffed the money into the sack, Elizabeth tried to think of what to do next. She never intended for her trip to the bank to turn out like this.

The whistle from the Southern Pacific four-ten pierced the silence in the room. The train was arriving at the station. She had to move quickly. From the other room came a teller's voice. "Mr. Pound, shall I close the vault now?"

Through the office door Elizabeth could see the open vault, about the size of a small closet. That was it.

"Mr. Pound, I'd like everybody in the vault," she said. There was no resistance. She was surprised at the power of a small pistol. Miss Ruther and the two tellers moved quickly over the wide threshold into the small room lined with shelves and a cabinet of small drawers. Pound entered last and now was even angrier at the humiliation of being locked in his own vault. He glared furiously at Elizabeth and remained silent.

"Sorry about the inconvenience, folks," Elizabeth said. "You'll be missed by suppertime and someone will come to let you out. I presume that's an air vent above the door, Mr. Pound. You can tell your rescuers the combination."

Elizabeth leaned her body against the massive door and managed to start it moving. She kept pushing until it closed with a thud and the bolts clunked solidly in place. She gave the combination dial a playful spin. Her happy mood surprised her. She had just robbed a bank.

Elizabeth stepped out onto the boardwalk and glanced about. Tucson on a bright July afternoon looked normal enough. There were a few people walking along in front of the shops and only light traffic of horses and wagons in the street.

With deliberate casualness, Elizabeth opened her parasol, cradled the sack of money in her arms, and strolled toward the train station three blocks away.

The train had arrived. She could see the puffs of steam rising above the buildings at the end of the street. She fought the urge to hurry. She could not afford to attract attention.

But attention usually followed Elizabeth Castle wherever she went. She was a beautiful woman, twenty-three years old, slender, with a delicately thin face. Her copper-red hair shone brightly in the afternoon sun as she walked along nodding cordially to the shoppers. Her fashionable green dress gently swept the boardwalk.

The world seemed so normal. It was hard for her to believe what just had happened. Now all her plans had to be changed.

As she approached the station platform she saw the other

four members of the show troupe pacing about and talking excitedly to the conductor. They were a whirl of dresses and hats and parasols.

Elizabeth relaxed when she saw them. They were more than her partners on the stage. They also were her friends. They had been through much together during the past two years. There was Katherine Barrons from St. Louis, the shortest of the group at five feet, with nut-brown hair and a nose that turned up slightly. Frances Roark was the youngest at nineteen and unhappy about having freckles. She thought they made her look childish. Her light blond hair fell about her face like fine corn silk.

Lou Coleman was another blonde, with a solid body that she called dumpy. Her angelic round face made her look much younger than her twenty-six years. And Rosa de la Garza was a Mexican beauty with coal-black hair and skin the soft brown of a young doe. They all could sing and dance, and Lou could make the saddest miner smile with her foot-stomping piano music.

When the girls spotted Elizabeth, they gave a cheer and waved for her to hurry. The train brakes hissed steam. She stepped into the bustle and chatter and said loudly, "Be quiet and listen to me." Calmly, quickly, she told them, "I may be suspected of robbing the bank. If you go with me you may be suspected of being accomplices. Stay here if you think you should. I'll send your back pay to you."

The girls were stunned. Her stern face told them she wasn't joking. Lou spoke for them all. "Liz, if we're bank robbers, let's act like it and get out of here." Laughing, they all climbed the steps, and the train began chugging westward.

When they pulled into Cortaro, about fifteen miles from Tucson, Elizabeth nervously looked out at the station platform. Sooner or later the Tucson marshal would telegraph the stations along the way, and at one of the stops they would be arrested.

A conference with the girls produced a plan. They would stay on the train until just before dark, when the bank people probably would be discovered. Then the girls would get off, buy a wagon and team, and head for Mexico. Rosa's father had a small ranch near Nogales, where they could stay until things cooled off. The plan sounded just simple enough to work.

About two hours after leaving Tucson, the train arrived at Black Springs, a bustling railroad town. The conductor told them Black Springs had two hotels, several rooming houses, a saloon called Chelsey's, a blacksmith shop with a livery stable, and various general stores and shops. He added that the town had a fine marshal named Earl Brenner.

Elizabeth was happy to see that this fine marshal had not arranged a reception party for them at the station. Maybe Alfred Pound, in spite of his anger at being locked in his own vault, wouldn't report what had happened. He knew she had a right to the money. Maybe he wanted to avoid an investigation.

Quickly the women got off the train. They arranged to have most of their baggage containing their stage costumes shipped on to San Francisco. They would hardly be needing them in Mexico.

Elizabeth followed the station agent's directions to the livery stable about four blocks away while the others headed for a hotel.

At the stable she found a short, heavy-set man with massive, glistening arms pounding at an anvil beside a glowing forge. He was dark with straight black hair chopped off at about jaw level. She thought he might be a Papago Indian; she had seen some of them occasionally in Tucson.

"Pardon me, I'd like to buy a two-horse team and a wagon."

The man did not break his rhythm of ringing blows, nor did he look up.

"I said I need . . ."

"He heard you, ma'am, but you'll have to wait a minute."

Elizabeth jumped when she heard the voice out of the darkness behind the door. As her eyes became more accustomed to the dim light, she made out a ranch hand sitting back on his heels. His eyes squinted against the smoke curling from the cigarette dangling from his lips.

"Jake's making a shoe for my horse right now. Besides, he don't talk even when he ain't working." The cowpuncher took a drag on his cigarette. "It's not that he won't talk, but he just can't. Had his tongue cut out. Some folks say it's a tribal custom."

"Oh, that s terrible!" She couldn't stop herself from saying it. She stole a quick glance at the blacksmith, who was plunging the shoe in a water tank. He was looking back at her.

The puncher laughed. "Don't let it bother you none, ma'am. At least he can hear real good." He laughed again as she blushed with embarrassment.

"If you're shopping for a team and rig," he said seriously, "I've got just what you want right outside the door there."

She had noticed the bay mare and a slightly smaller buckskin hitched to a two-seater buckboard. She looked closer at the horses now. They seemed fit.

"How much do you want?" she asked.

"Well, I'm trying to trade them to Jake for some high-priced horseflesh out in the corral, but he's not in a trading mood today." The man lifted his hat and scratched his head. "How about a hundred and eighty dollars?"

She had never bought a team and rig before. She glanced at Jake, hoping for a clue of some sort. The blacksmith was standing beside his anvil watching them, his heavy arms folded across his chest. His face didn't reveal a thing.

She had seen her father trade horses. She would have to rely on memory, a little intuition, and a lot of bluff.

"The buckskin looks a bit stunted to me," she said, "and I'm not sure they're a good match. I'd have to give them a run."

"You're welcome to try, ma'am," he said, grinning at her.

She climbed onto the seat and wrapped the reins around each hand the way her father had taught her. She was glad she had grown up driving his teams. With a shout, she headed the team out across a meadow bordering the edge of town. She ran them about a half mile and then back, tied the reins, and climbed down.

"They feel okay for a short run, but I'm still not sure they'll last for the long haul. I'll give you one hundred twenty." She wasn't too sure about prices, but she knew the puncher expected to take advantage of her. He seemed less arrogant now, even somewhat irritated.

"Ma'am, you'd be stealing them from me at that price, for sure." He was almost whining. "How about a hundred sixty?"

She looked once again at Jake, who still had a stone face. She reached in her purse and pulled out some bills. "Here's one hundred and forty and that's it." She thrust the money toward the man. "And that's only if you throw in that carbine under the seat."

The cowpuncher winced. "Lady, you're a coldhearted trader. But I guess it's a deal." He took the money.

Her look at Jake this time caught a slight nod and a smile. She turned toward him. "Will you feed and stable them tonight? I'll come by for them at sunrise."

Jake nodded again and Elizabeth headed for the hotel, leaving the cowpuncher counting his money, his eyes still squinting against the smoke.

Seth March poked stiffly at the coals under the coffeepot as the warmth of the sun's first rays soaked into his shivering body. In southern Arizona Territory it was the early morning Seth liked best, especially in the summer. The cool of the dawn and the soft first light of the sun could help a man forgive the heat and dust of the day before. It also could help him forget his worries.

He watched with satisfaction as the mist rose from the valley floor. He was camped on a knoll about two hundred feet above a creek crossing. Sandstone Creek was running full now because of the rains. In another month it would be dry. Black Mountain rose on the horizon to the east. The Santa Cruz Rivervalley ran south toward Tucson and north toward the town of Black Springs.

Seth's Appaloosa whinnied and tugged on her halter as she turned toward a ridge to the north. He stood and faced that way, too. He heard the muffled pounding of hooves before he saw the buckboard emerge from a draw about a quarter mile away.

The rig was being driven hard and from the way the team was straining he could tell it was tired. The right horse seemed to be favoring one leg slightly. Two people were on the front seat and three in the back.

As the wagon crossed the creek below his camp, he could see, to his surprise, that all the passengers were women. The rig rattled up the rocky road toward his camp. The horses were lathered and blowing hard. With brakes screeching on the iron rims, the buckboard cut sharply to the left and stopped right in front of him.

The dust quickly caught up with them. In the swirl he couldn't believe his squinting eyes. Every one of the women was young and attractive and dressed up fit to kill. A couple of them were even beautiful.

The driver was in her early twenties, with copper-red hair spilling out from under a wide-brimmed straw hat. The reins were wrapped several times around her small hands. Obviously she was in command.

"Mister, one of our horses threw a shoe and is about to go lame. Trade horses with us and we'll give you twenty dollars to boot."

"Sorry, ma'am, I don't have much use for a lame horse." He raised his coffee cup and gestured toward the pot on the fire. "You're welcome to some coffee."

The driver leaned forward in the seat. "We're not here to socialize. We swap our mare for your Appaloosa and give you fifty dollars. Now, that's more than fair."

The woman nervously fidgeted with the reins, and two of the others were looking back at the ridge.

"That's a generous offer but, as I said, a lame mount won't do me much good out here. I'm sorry. Maybe you can make it back into Black Springs and get her shod."

He glanced back at the ridge trying to guess what they were afraid of. When he returned his gaze to the driver, he was looking into a carbine she had leveled at his eyes. She looked determined.

"We don't have time to bargain, mister. We're taking the horse."

Seth nodded and gestured toward his horse. "I never argue with a rifle. What's mine is yours."

The driver gave orders and three of the women got down and began changing the team. Another rummaged around in a cotton sack on the floor of the buckboard. She counted out fifty dollars and handed the money to Seth on her way to help the others.

He continued sipping the coffee with his eyes fixed on the driver. She was beautiful, all right. Her green eyes could pierce right through a man. She glanced back at the ridge, checked the women's progress with the horses, and then looked back at the ridge again.

He found the whole scene entertaining and knew he must be crazy to think so. This woman was leaving him a lame horse, and she was so nervous she might shoot him at any second. Yet he couldn't resist teasing her.

"Sure you can't stay and join me for a cup of coffee?"

She looked at him quickly. She seemed surprised that he was joking at a time like this. He thought he detected the beginnings of a smile, a longing to laugh, to tease back, but her answer was stern.

"All right. It's no secret. We're running. But we didn't do anything wrong. That's why we need your help. If you must know, we are all the wives of a man, a Mormon, who was jailed in Black Springs. We are always being persecuted just because we're different."

"Yes, ma'am, I'd say five wives is different," he said.

"You see, our husband told us to try to make it to a Mormon settlement west of here before we are arrested too, or maybe even . . . taken advantage of . . . because we are alone and unprotected." She lowered her gaze to the ground. She seemed to be embarrassed by her last remark.

She hardly looked defenseless and unprotected to Seth as she sat there pointing the rifle at him. He suspected some playacting but wasn't sure how much. The others were finished changing the horses.

"I'm sure sorry about your troubles, ma'am, but you've got a good horse now. Maybe you'll try my coffee next time."

"Next time for sure, cowboy. Thanks for the swap." With a flurry and a rustle of dresses and ribbons and petticoats the women climbed aboard the wagon.

Suddenly one of them said softly, "Oh, no. They're already here."

Everyone turned quickly toward the ridge about a mile to the north. Several riders had topped the rise. Even at that distance it was obvious they were riding hard.

"Let's get out of here, Liz!" shouted another woman, clearly frightened. For a moment the driver watched the riders approach. When they veered toward Seth's camp it was clear they had seen the buckboard and the women.

The driver put down the rifle and dragged out the white sack stuffed as full as a feather pillow and tied near the top with a red ribbon. She pushed the sack over the side of the wagon. It landed at his feet with a heavy plop.

"Take care of that for us, mister, and we'll make it worth your while." Her eyes met his for just a second. They didn't show pleading, just hope. Then with a lurch the buckboard rattled off as the driver shouted at the horses and snapped the reins against their backs. They headed south on the trail that followed the stream. One of the women turned and gave him a quick smile and a wave before grabbing hold of the seat to keep from bouncing off.

Seth had to think fast. Should he leave the sack where it was and be no party to this? Or should he hide it? The riders were out of sight now, crossing the bottom of the draw. When they topped the next hill they would be able to see his every move. It had to be now or not at all.

In a sweeping motion, he reached down with his left hand and on the backswing pitched the sack into the brush behind his bedroll and saddle. It was heavier than he expected, and he was afraid it hadn't gone far enough.

The riders emerged from the draw just then. Seth didn't dare look back to see if the sack had fallen out of view. He took another sip from the cup, which he still held in his right hand. The coffee now was too cool to drink, but he needed something to cover his nervousness.

He felt his heart pounding as he watched the four horses splash across the creek. It was a posse, no question about it.

The marshal was an old-timer who looked as if he had seen better days. Two of the other men were dressed like ranch hands in canvas trousers and vests. The fourth man, softer and younger, was dressed in a gray suit and derby. He probably was a shopkeeper or a clerk in town.

The marshal pulled up hard in front of Seth and waved the others on. "Walk 'em for a ways and give 'em a breather, then get that rig. I'll catch up to you."

The big man looked down at Seth, measuring him from his hat to his boots. The marshal's face was a map of deep creases and his mouth was covered by a drooping, snow-white moustache. His sweat-soaked shirt was caked with dust.

"We saw you talking to those women. What's your name and what are you doing here?"

"Name's Seth March and I'm just passing through."

"I'm Earl Brenner, Black Springs marshal." He shifted his weight in the saddle. "I could take you in on suspicion of being in cahoots with that bunch, March. You know a good reason why I shouldn't?"

"I never saw those ladies before in my life, Marshal. They took my horse but wouldn't stay for coffee. Must have known you were coming."

"They knew, all right," the marshal muttered.

"What do you want them for? The story they told me doesn't account for all this hard riding."

"That figures," the marshal said. "They've been fooling a lot of folks around here. Probably told you they were going to a church social." He gave a loud, raucous laugh that ended with a coughing fit. He gasped for air. When he recovered, he said in a growling voice, "They robbed a bank in Tucson, that's all they did."

Seth gave a low whistle and hoped again the sack had fallen out of sight. He watched Brenner's eyes as they made a sweep of his campsite. The old man didn't seem to suspect anything.

Seth took another sip of cold coffee. "If you catch them, Marshal, the Appaloosa was mine. I'd like to trade back."

"We'll catch 'em, all right. And I want to talk to you again. Don't get too far away."

"I won't get far on a lame horse," Seth said.

Brenner spurred his mount into a gallop in the direction in which the others had gone. As soon as he was out of sight, Seth found the sack behind a clumb of scrub oak. He knelt down, quickly untied the red ribbon, and looked inside.

A chill ran across his shoulders. The sack was filled with money neatly wrapped in bundles. Printed on each wrapper were the words, "Tucson Cattlemen's Bank."

CHAPTER 2

ELIZABETH Castle wasn't sure why she decided to leave the money with the stranger. Maybe it was because she had little choice, or maybe there was something about the way he looked or talked.

He was a handsome man, no doubt about that. He was tall and lanky, and his deeply tanned face and square jaw gave him a rugged look. There also was a gentle look about him that was harder to describe. It was reflected in his teasing, dark brown eyes.

Brown hair curled out from under his battered, wide-brimmed hat. He wore a dingy shirt and a leather vest. His gun belt hung loosely from his narrow hips.

It wasn't just his appearance that had caused her to throw off the money so impulsively. It was something about his manner. He seemed to be a man who valued independence and who made up his own mind about things. He wouldn't jump to conclusions about five women and a bag full of money. At least she hoped he wouldn't.

She didn't have time to wonder about that now nor even to wonder what he would do with the money.

The wagon road continued to follow the creek. She slowed the team for a rest and looked over her shoulder again for the posse. Her father had told her that learning to drive a team would come in handy one day. He was right.

But she doubted he was talking about a day like this had turned out to be.

A few hours earlier she and the other girls had awakened just about at sunrise. From the stairway landing in the hotel they had overheard the station agent talking to the desk clerk. A telegram telling of the bank robbery had arrived from Tucson. It described her and said she was traveling by train with four other women. The agent had not been able to find the marshal.

The desk clerk began whispering something to the agent. Elizabeth knew it had to be about her and the other girls. Five women together don't check into a small-town hotel unnoticed.

She sent the others back to the rooms to get the bags and the money. Then she took a deep breath, fixed a smile on her face, and breezed cheerfully down the stairs. She greeted the startled men at the desk and strolled casually out the hotel entranceway.

When she reached the boardwalk, she sauntered out of sight, then walked quickly, almost running, toward the livery stable. The team was harnessed and waiting. She climbed to the seat and gathered the reins.

Then she looked up and almost screamed. Jake was standing beside the bay holding the bridle. He must have heard about the telegram and was trying to stop her. She glanced down at the buckboard floor. The carbine still was there.

The big blacksmith must have sensed her desperation. He smiled and held up a hand to calm her. Then he leaned over and lifted the right forefoot of the mare. He pointed to the shoe and wiggled it slightly to show that it was loose.

She felt foolish about her fear. "Thanks, Jake, but I don't have time to get her shod."

He looked at her quizzically and let the leg drop. He

stepped back out of the way. She knew, just as he did, that it might be harmful to the horse, but she had no choice. She had to get out of Black Springs.

She paid Jake for stabling the horses and picked up the girls at the hotel back stairs. By the time they reached the edge of Black Springs, the town was waking up. Several men saw them heading out. It was just a matter of time before the marshal received the message and put a posse on their trail.

It must have happened quickly because now the posse had almost caught up with them. Her horses were galloping again, but she knew they couldn't keep up the pace much longer.

Up ahead she saw a small waterfall where the streambed dropped down about six feet. A pool had formed at the base of the fall. It looked inviting. The horses were kicking up dust, and already the morning was getting hot. But she couldn't think about comforts such as a cool swim now.

The others saw the pool, too. "I could sure use a bath about now," said Frances.

"That just shows you crime doesn't pay, Freckles," said Lou. "Now, if we weren't bank robbers, we could stop here and get out of these clothes and . . ."

"That's it!" Elizabeth shouted. She drove the team off the road and reined them to a halt near the falls. "We can't outrun the posse. And if that cowboy decides to help, he'll need some time."

Elizabeth was already out of the buckboard and halfway out of her dress. "Everybody strip and get in the pool. Hand down that rifle, Kate. Maybe it will work for us again."

Dresses, petticoats, shoes, and stockings started flying and soon covered the creekbank.

"Okay, girls," Elizabeth said, "we've come for a swimming party. Make it look good." She jumped into the pool.

They saw the three men in the posse pull up short about fifty yards from the wagon. The men drew their revolvers and slowly approached. By the time they reached the pool, their astonishment was obvious. The five desperate outlaws had become a pool full of women splashing and laughing and chattering. Embarrassed, the men holstered their pistols.

"Good morning, gentlemen," Elizabeth said. "Don't you have better manners than to stare at ladies taking a bath?" The men awkwardly looked at each other and then looked back down the road for the marshal.

One of them cleared his throat. "You ladies are wanted for bank robbery," he said. He had a crooked nose and nervously fingered his moustache. "And the marshal says we're supposed to take you in."

"Hey, mister," said Lou, "why are you being so serious? I'll bet you've got a real cute smile."

The thin man next to him chuckled, "Say, Luke, I think you've made a friend."

"Any law against coming out here for a swim?" Elizabeth asked.

The man named Luke looked at her for a moment, then said to the thin man, "Walter, that stream is pretty cold. I'll bet if we just wait long enough these ladies will start freezing. Then they'll have to come out."

"Now, wouldn't that be an eyeful," said Walter. "I'd be willing to sit all day for a sight like that."

"Marshal Brenner's coming," the smaller man in a suit said with obvious relief.

The marshal reined in next to the others. "What the devil is this, Luke? You ladies are going back to town. Get out of that creek." He dismounted stiffly and walked toward them.

"Marshal, you may be the law, but that doesn't entitle

you to take liberties," Elizabeth said. "We're not getting out of the water until you get out of sight." She managed an angry glare.

Marshal Brenner was flustered. "Now just a minute, missy, you're not giving orders here." He surveyed the clothes-strewn bank and eyed the wagon. "All right, you men search the wagon and look through these clothes for the money and for guns." The search turned up neither money nor guns.

"Let's have it," Brenner said. "Where's the money?"

"Okay, Marshal, you'd guess it sooner or later, so we might as well tell you." Elizabeth gave a resigned smile. "It's in the bottom of this creek. A few rocks in the sack and down it went."

It was a stupid story, but it was the best she could think of quickly. It might buy some time.

"I wouldn't bet eight eggs on finding the money in that creek," Brenner said, "but we have to look." He turned to his men. "Luke, can you swim?" The marshal didn't wait for a reply. "Get in there and check out the bottom."

He turned to the women. "Okay, ladies, get out."

"As I said, Marshal," Elizabeth replied, "you men will at least have to turn your backs. We're very shy."

"I can tell how shy you are," Brenner mumbled. "Make it snappy." Then he motioned for the men to turn and face the road.

She signaled the other women to move to the side of the pool. She quickly climbed out on the bank away from the road, reached into the high grass, and brought out the rifle.

"Okay, boys, you can turn around now." She read the surprise on their faces as they saw her standing there dripping wet in a full-length white chemise, holding the rifle on them.

"Marshal," Walter said slowly, "I hope nobody rides by right now. I'll bet we look damn silly."

"Lady, you shoot one of us and everybody else draws on you." Brenner was concerned. "Some people are going to get killed. Don't be stupid."

She realized she may have miscalculated. This move had seemed like a good stall for time and therefore a worthwhile risk. But now she could see the danger of the situation. She wanted very much to be out of the predicament and away from there. She longed to be with her grandfather in St. Louis or singing in a theater. She vowed not to cry or look weak.

"You win, Marshal. I'm putting the rifle down." She placed the gun carefully on the bank and began wading back into the pool. "And you're right, too, Luke. You did look pretty silly." She was glad when the other women laughed so she could laugh with them.

Brenner sent the men to search the area away from the pool while the women put on their dresses over sopping-wet undergarments. Then everyone watched while Luke began diving and searching the creekbed under the falls.

After about fifteen minutes, Luke sat on the bank, gasping. Then Walter and the other men floundered about in the water trying to feel the bottom with their feet.

"I don't know where that money is, ladies," Brenner said, "but it's not in that water. Let's get back to town."

"At least the morning's not a complete loss, Marshal," Kate teased. "You've got five dangerous criminals and the cleanest posse in the territory."

As the group passed Seth's camp on the trip back to Black Springs, Elizabeth looked for signs of the money. At first she saw nothing. A blackened spot on the ground caused by the campfire was the only sign that anyone had been there. Maybe he simply grabbed the money and took off.

Then she spied a patch of fresh earth higher up the slope above the campsite. It looked like a hole had been dug recently, a hole about the size of a stuffed sack.

*   *   *

The sun was high overhead by the time Seth March had crossed the creek on his way to Black Springs. He smiled as he thought back to that time when he was about nine years old and his father had made him walk around for a whole day with a pebble in his boot. After a stone had embedded in the frog of his pony's hoof, Seth had forced the pony to keep running. His father believed punishment should teach a lesson.

Seth had learned his lesson well. After that he always could tell when a horse had picked up a stone. That woman driving the buckboard had been right about the mare's thrown shoe. But it was a stone that was making the horse limp. After he dug out the stone with his knife, he knew the horse could carry him the eight miles to Black Springs with little problem.

The midmorning heat sent shimmering waves rising from the scrub grass and the mesquite trees. It was a pleasant ride, except he was annoyed by the lingering realization that he was in trouble.

He couldn't explain why he hadn't turned over the money to Marshal Brenner. After the marshal rode off, Seth had stuffed the money into the hollow of a cottonwood tree. He never had stolen in his life. Furthermore, he didn't care that much for the things that money could buy.

The image of that woman holding the rifle came drifting back to him. He had not been able to get her out of his mind all morning. One particular picture stayed in the front of his memory. It was that moment when just a slight smile flickered across her face. She had wanted to laugh, to relax, to enjoy the conversation.

Why did that particular picture of her return? He knew, of course, as soon as he asked the question. It was Louise. She was the reason for the persistent image.

He had been caught off guard by the events of the

morning. It had been three years since he had been around women who acted and dressed as these women, fashionable and apparently refined.

A fleeting image of Louise on their wedding day crossed his mind. The pain high in his chest began. He knew what would come next. There'd be the gnawing in his stomach and then he'd be unable to take a deep breath for a while.

For the thousandth time he reached into his vest pocket and pulled out the photograph. It was taken on their wedding day. Louise was standing beside the chair wanting to laugh but resisting the impulse. She looked stern because the photographer had ordered them to be still.

Seth had seen that expression again a few hours earlier at the creek crossing. It was the same longing to laugh behind a stern face. That had set it off.

Now came the memory of Louise in the kitchen just after he had teased her about something, maybe about her cooking. Her laughter and playful threats were vivid. He knew the joy of that laughter, the laughter she was trying to hold back in front of the camera, the laughter which did explode as soon as the photographer said, "That's it."

That memory made the stern expression in the photograph even more painful. Blond hair neatly packed into a bun rested on the back of her head and neck, leaving her thin, pale neck so beautiful and vulnerable. She held her chin high.

He sat beside her stiffly and proudly, so satisfied, in a borrowed wedding suit. Even while seated, Seth at six feet, two inches was almost as tall as Louise standing beside him.

His soft brown hair was slicked down for the picture. He had changed little in physical appearance since that photograph was taken three years ago. The lines in his face were a little deeper, and the long days in the saddle had left their mark on his sun-toughened skin.

Louise used to tease him about being so handsome that he

nearly made women faint. He never thought of himself in that way. As he looked at the picture one more time before putting it away, he saw a beautiful woman, and beside her sat a foolish man dressed up in clothes that made him look like somebody else in some other time.

He had lived up to that foolish image this time. It had been stupid to hide the money. But he felt almost bewitched by that redhead.

Black Springs now was about a mile ahead. He could find a blacksmith to shoe the mare and then get some supplies. To hell with that woman. He'd leave a note at the marshal's office telling him where he could find the money. Then Seth could continue his trip west to the San Joaquin Valley and his land. Three years was too long to be away. Most important of all, he had not yet said good-bye to Louise.

CHAPTER 3

THE waitress banged down a plate heaped with sliced beef and brown beans and a cup of steaming coffee. "The name's Molly," she said loudly. "Just holler if you want more. I like to see a man eat hearty."

Seth watched the cheerful, stout woman move from table to table laughing with her customers. The scene made him feel at home in Black Springs. It was a reminder that most people are honest and decent and want to get along with others. Even those five women probably had some good reason for running with a sackful of money.

He smiled at himself. He was getting soft. It came with deciding to head back to California and with thinking about Louise again. She always had had that effect upon him, making him see the good in the world and giving people the benefit of the doubt.

He also knew that kind of thinking could get a man killed in this territory. Being skeptical was not always just a philosophy of life. Sometimes it was necessary for survival. Something seemed to be saying to him now that survival was at stake and he'd better toughen up. Forget those women, get the note to the marshal, and get out of town.

He glanced out the window and saw that his warning thoughts had come too late. Across the street from the cafe the wagonload of women and the posse had just pulled up at the marshal's office. Marshal Brenner looked tired and irritable. Townsfolk gathered around and kidded the posse about bringing in such vicious outlaws. The women appeared calm and confident.

He felt stirrings of admiration for the five ladies. It had taken the posse half the day to bring them in. The women must have given them trouble, probably to give him time to hide the money. The marshal was no fool either.

Seth had to play his hand very carefully. Most of the other players were smart and, as he already found out, they didn't mind bluffing. The stakes were high for some. His next move was to tell the women he was leaving the game.

By the time he finished his lunch, the crowd across the street had drifted away. He walked over and entered the marshal's office. The women had been locked in cells in a long room at the back. A heavy oak door to the cell room stood open.

The office was furnished roughly and simply with a pot-bellied stove, a scratched-up wooden desk cluttered with paper, two solid chairs next to the desk and, near the door, a gun rack holding six or seven rifles. The windows were fly-specked and dusty. The floor was tracked with dirt.

Marshal Brenner recognized him. "I was wondering what happened to you. As I remember, your name's March."

"That's right, Marshal. I decided to come on in and wait for my horse. Looks like it took you a while."

Brenner swore quietly. "A lot of people couldn't wait till Saturday for their baths. The boys took your Appaloosa over to the stable. Are we going to have to add horse stealing to the robbery charges?"

"Nothing like that," Seth said quickly. "It was a trade with money to boot. I'd just like to trade back now."

Brenner pulled out a bandanna and wiped the sweat and dust off his face. "I suppose that would be all right, but you'll have to talk with those women, and I'll have to hold any money involved until after the hearing."

The back room was three cells and a passageway within solid stone walls. Four small windows near the ceiling did little to cool off the stifling heat. Each cell had two beds made of wooden platforms covered by thin mattresses and rough wool blankets.

Seth could tell that the women were relieved to see him, but the redhead played it cool. "Well, cowboy, how did you like my mare?" Her eyes were playful. She was more beautiful than Seth remembered, even though her dress now was rumpled and muddy and her hair was caked with dust.

"That mare is a fine horse, ma'am, but since you're down on your luck right now, my conscience just won't let me take advantage of you. I'm willing to swap back. By the way, my name's Seth March."

"I'm Elizabeth Castle. That's Lou Coleman and Frances Roark in the cell next door, and in the guest room next to them are Kate Barrons and Rosa de la Garza."

The women said hello and seemed to be in good spirits. He could tell they were eager to ask about the money.

"Now, about this horse swapping . . ." Elizabeth began loudly, then quietly asked, "What about the money?" All five waited eagerly for his answer.

"Sorry to disappoint you, ladies, but I'm going to tell the marshal where I hid it. Then I'm heading out."

"Wait a minute, March. You can't do that. We trusted you with that money." Elizabeth no longer was cool and aloof.

They all heard someone enter the marshal's office. They couldn't make out the muffled conversation that followed.

Seth stepped closer to the bars and spoke softly, "Look, Miss Castle, you didn't trust me. You had no choice. You just dumped that money out of desperation. And I'm not entirely sure why I hid it."

He had to look away. Her green eyes were pleading for help. He remembered again the way she had looked earlier that morning, beautiful and vulnerable and wanting to laugh. This was tougher than he had expected.

"I can't get tangled up in anything illegal," he said, "especially now."

"But you don't understand. I didn't . . ." Elizabeth stopped talking, shrugged slightly, and sighed. "Forget it. The story sounds ridiculous. You wouldn't believe it." She stared silently at the floor.

"Well, I'll tell him," Lou blurted out. "There's nothing illegal in this, Mr. March, and that money wasn't really stolen. That money belonged to Liz. She was just getting back what was rightly hers."

"That's true," said Kate. "It was the bank that broke the law. They tried to keep her money when the court said she could have it."

Frances chimed in, "Liz just had to persuade them a little, and . . . well, it took a gun to do it. Now, I don't think . . ."

"Pulling a gun in a bank and taking out money sounds like bank robbery to me," Seth interrupted. He wasn't sure what to make of all this. He wanted to believe that they were innocent, but he wouldn't let them trick him. They were admitting the money was taken by force. He had to challenge their story.

"If you can't tell a more believable tale than that, I don't want to throw in with you. That's about as believable as the one about being Mormon wives." He looked at Elizabeth, who began to blush.

"All right, Mr. March," she said, "so you don't believe us. But you can't get out now. You're in with us, like it or not."

She had regained her composure. Her smile was the smile of a fox. He was afraid he knew what was coming next.

"You try to weasel out of this, Mr. March, and we'll put on a real show." Elizabeth stepped back and made a sweeping gesture toward the other women.

"Ladies and gentlemen"—she cleared her throat dramatically—"I present to you five young, innocent girls who were tricked into pulling a bank robbery for a no-good skunk of a man who then took the money and turned them in." She gave a deep bow as the other women applauded and laughed.

Elizabeth pressed her face against the bars and spoke quietly. "Think about it, Seth. You're the one linked to the money if you tell the marshal where it is. Who's he going to believe then?" She gave him a cunning smile.

He didn't doubt she was serious. She wasn't through.

"You help us escape and return the money to us, and we go our separate ways. But until then, we're partners, partner." Her voice was cheerful. She seemed to enjoy blackmail. Or maybe she just wanted to see him squirm.

He knew she was right. He had no choice. But he didn't want them to know that yet.

Elizabeth still spoke sweetly. "And after all this is over, you've got a share coming if you want it." She smiled. "But to you, of course, it'll be stolen money." The others laughed.

"And I thought you drove a hard bargain with that horse swap," he said. These women were beautiful and dangerous. He had to think things over. "Don't go away, ladies. I'll let you know." Without another word, he turned and walked out.

As Seth stepped back into Brenner's office, he sensed tension in the air. Brenner had company. The man was tall, about six-two, and powerfully built. He wore a black, tailor-made suit and a white shirt. His flat-crowned leather hat was pulled low over his dark, deep-set eyes. For some reason his face seemed slightly unbalanced. Then Seth saw that part of his left ear was missing. A black leather holster, almost covered by his coat, hung high on his left hip.

The man turned toward Seth and spoke with a hoarse voice, "Is your name March?"

"That's right. And you?" Seth held out his hand. The man ignored it.

"Roscoe Kirby. I represent the Tucson Cattlemen's Bank. I'm here to take those robbers and the money back to Tucson."

"Kirby's a bounty hunter, Seth," Brenner said, glaring at the man. "And he was just leaving."

Kirby looked at the marshal coldly and turned again toward Seth. "I understand you talked to those women out on the trail and you've seen them just now. What's your connection with them?"

"You don't have to answer, Seth," Brenner said. "We'll have a legal hearing for that."

Arrogance always had irritated Seth and he instantly took a dislike to Kirby. "It's okay, Marshal. I have nothing to hide." He smiled at Kirby pleasantly. "This morning these women told me they were Mormons and I came here this afternoon to pray with them."

Kirby sneered and moved toward Seth. "You got a smart mouth, March."

"That's enough, Kirby," Brenner snapped, standing quickly. "You have no jurisdiction here. The last thing I need right now is a hungry bounty hunter pretending to be the law." Brenner began coughing and had to grab the desk for support.

Kirby adjusted his gun belt. "You need more than that, old man. You're the one pretending to be the law. You haven't got breath or guts enough to handle this case. I'm telling you to turn those women over to me so I can take them to Tucson."

Brenner recovered from his coughing fit. Angrily, he stepped up toe to toe with Kirby. In a controlled, growling voice, almost a whisper Seth could barely hear, Brenner said, "Get the hell out of here, bounty hunter, or so help me, you'll never leave."

The two stood like wild animals trying to face each other down. Seth knew immediately he would have to side with the marshal if Kirby didn't back off. Seth couldn't let this bounty hunter have the women. He was surprised by his feelings. These women were blackmailing him, and yet he felt protective toward them.

Kirby must have sensed Seth's intentions. He glanced at Seth, then looked back at Brenner. After a few more seconds, Kirby broke the silence. "One way or another, I'll get what I came for."

He backed slowly toward the door and opened it. He looked at Seth. "I'm not through with you, March." The windows rattled when the door slammed.

Brenner let out a deep sigh. "He's gonna be trouble. Watch out for him, Seth. Bounty hunters like that would even drag themselves in if the reward were high enough."

Seth knew he had not seen the last of Roscoe Kirby.

CHAPTER 4

MARSHAL Brenner eased back in his chair. "I guess we'd better go over your story again, March. These women, confound them, they didn't have the money when we caught up with them. Tell me once more what you know."

Seth was pretty sure Brenner didn't suspect him of anything. The marshal was just trying to get the story straight. His confrontation with Kirby a few minutes earlier had left Brenner uneasy.

"As I told you this morning, Marshal, when the women . . ."

The sound of gunfire from the street startled them both. Brenner stood quickly. "Probably that damn bounty hunter stirring up trouble." Seth followed Brenner out on the boardwalk.

In the middle of the dusty street a young man about eighteen or nineteen was sitting a skittish roan horse. His pistol was drawn. Obviously he had been drinking. About twenty yards down the street stood the Indian blacksmith Seth had left the mare with for shoeing.

"What's going on out here?" Brenner shouted at the young man.

"Just leave me be, Marshal!" the man shouted back with the slur and swagger of a drunk. "I'm just about to kill me an Injun!" The blacksmith stood unarmed, still and silent.

"Put it away, mister," Brenner said. "There'll be no kill-ing here." Then he shouted toward the blacksmith, "You okay, Jake?" The Indian nodded once and remained standing in the street.

"This is something I gotta do, Marshal!" the gunman shouted. "I just found out my brother's dead. They say he got killed by some Papagos. Looks like he died real slow. I aim to even things up."

"I'm sorry about your brother, but you're just making trouble for yourself. This won't bring him back. Go home, son, and sleep it off." A crowd was gathering and Brenner motioned for the people to stay out of the way.

The man climbed off his horse and gave it a slap. It trotted away a few steps. The man then took a wide stance, his right hand hanging near his holstered pistol.

"You're an Injun-lover, Marshal. I'm gonna get that savage even if I have to take you first."

Brenner spoke calmly. "Boy, if you don't leave now I'll have to lock you up."

The man drew and shot out a pane of glass in the window to the left of Brenner's head, then he fired another shot. The tinkle of falling glass continued after the echoes of the gun-fire were silent.

Seth stood about ten feet to the right of Brenner. Seth watched the old man's jaw muscles tighten in his tired face. The marshal's voice was tired, too, weary of all of this.

"I've looked at so many of you kids over the end of my gun barrel, it makes me sick to think about it. I don't want to kill you, boy. Leave. Now."

Brenner moved toward the street, and another shot cracked the silence. A chip of wood flew off the step just in front of his boot. He continued down the steps without a pause.

The drunk man began crying. "Dolph was a good man,

and those redskins killed him. They killed a good man."
Brenner still was walking toward him, about six paces
away. He held out his hand for the pistol.

Tears were running down the young man's face as he
raised the gun. He fired. Brenner spun around and crashed
into the hitching rail, clutching his right shoulder.

The man clicked his empty revolver twice, then reached
down to his shell belt for another bullet. Jake started running toward him, and the man saw the big Indian coming.
Brenner pulled himself up. Supported by the hitching rail,
he tried to reach across his body with his left hand to draw
his gun. His face was twisted with pain.

The young man pulled a bullet out of his belt and tried to
see through his tears to load it into an empty chamber. He
rolled the chamber into place. Jake was nearly on him.

As the man swung the gun toward Jake, Seth felt his own
hand move up in a rhythmic, fluid sweep toward his own
pistol. He felt the handle lightly in place in his palm. As the
weight lifted out of the holster, his arm finished the swing
upward and leveled the revolver.

He saw the man's shirt jerk almost before he heard the
sharp crack of the gun and felt it jolt his arm. The man
looked confused. Then his eyes found Seth. He squeezed his
shot off at the ground and crumpled in the dust at Jake's
feet.

Jake stared at Seth without expression. Then the Indian
doubled his fist, struck his chest once, and extended his open
hand, palm up, toward Seth. Seth wasn't sure what the sign
language meant. Jake seemed to be saying thanks. Seth
nodded and the Indian turned and walked down the street
toward his shop.

The pungent odor of the gunpowder in the air was sharp
and exciting. Seth always associated it with times when his
nerves and muscles were alert, with times of survival. It
bothered him that it was an exciting smell because it usually

meant death. He thought of Louise again and felt weary to
the bone.

Brenner still was holding onto the hitching rail. The griz-
zled old man was as tough as anyone Seth had met. Brenner
looked up at Seth. "If that kid hadn't been crying, he could
have aimed better and saved me the trouble of retiring."

Brenner moved toward the steps. "Help me into the
office, Seth. I can't let anybody think a kid's slug can slow
me down." Seth steadied Brenner as he climbed the stairs to
the boardwalk.

"I guess I'm getting soft in my old age," Brenner said in a
grumbling voice. "I should have drawn on the kid, but I
thought I could keep him alive. I figured he'd fold and give
me the gun." He sighed deeply. "I'm really sick of the
killing. I guess that means it's time for me to hang it up, to
take off this badge."

By the time Seth had eased Brenner into his chair and had
poured the man a double shot of whiskey, the doctor
arrived. He plopped a leather bag on the desk and stared at
the marshal, his hands on his hips.

"You old fool," the doctor said loudly. "I've been telling
you for years this business is bad for your health." He began
opening Brenner's shirt.

"Seth, this here is Doc Sam McKinney. He's a horse doctor, but now and then we let him work on people."

The doctor busied himself with Brenner's shoulder
wound. McKinney was a small man about Brenner's age of
sixty. He was almost completely bald, with a fringe of white
hair around the sides and back of his head. He had a round
face, twinkling eyes, and wore a rumpled gray suit.

McKinney began probing gently for the bullet while
Brenner frowned. Seth could see that the bullet had entered
just below the collarbone. Sweat drops broke out on Brenner's forehead.

"I'll swear, Sam, I think that rumor about you and the

Indians is true." Brenner turned his head toward Seth. "They say this old quack lived with the Apache for a couple of years. He thought he was learning cures from their medicine men. But what he really saw was the Apache torturing their enemies. Now he's trying it on us civilized folks and we can't tell the difference either."

McKinney applied a compress to the wound and took a deep breath. "Looks like you'll live to get shot at another day, Earl. But I'll have to dig it out. Think you can make it to my office without dying on the way?"

McKinney turned to Seth with a solemn expression. "It always upsets the local folk to have their marshals dying in the streets."

"Sam, you think I'd let a fumbling old fool like you take a slug out of me?"

"If I'd kept all the slugs I've dug out of you over the years, Earl, this town could build a lead statue of its marshal as a tribute to stubbornness." He gestured to Seth. "Mr. March, would you help me drag our fine marshal over to my place?"

After he helped deliver Brenner to McKinney's office, Seth headed for the livery stable. He wanted to check on his Appaloosa. As he strolled along the boardwalk he watched the people shopping and riding by.

The rough affection the marshal and the doctor had for each other told of the stability of Black Springs. Trust and respect had built up over the years, even if they admitted it only by fussing and fuming with each other. Those two men represented the roots of this community.

It reminded him of Montrose, the town in California near his ranch in the San Joaquin Valley beyond the Sierra Nevadas. It was the town near where he and Louise had hoped to live and have neighbors like these people here.

He remembered the first time he had shown that land to Louise. That had been only three weeks after they were married in St. Louis. He had been back East to organize a wagon train.

He already had led three wagon trains from Missouri to California. He had carefully saved his earnings and had bought a section of prime rangeland in the northern San Joaquin Valley. It was a small tract of land compared to some of the huge ranches, but it was a start.

When he met Louise, he knew it was time to go back to settle on the land. The wagon train trip West usually took three or four months. This time it took him two weeks by buggy and train with his bride.

As they stood in the middle of a green meadow under a bright blue sky, they both knew they had found their place. It was good land for grazing, with plenty of water most of the year and abundant grass. The majestic Sierra Nevadas filled the eastern horizon, and the land rolled gently toward the San Joaquin River. The house would be built upon the rise overlooking the meadow and the river. The barn and the corral would be just to the north of the house.

But all that was to come later. Until they could build a shack for temporary shelter, they slept under the wagon. Seth's savings bought a small herd to begin with, and their dream was under way.

Then that first year brought a bad drought. The water dried up and the grass was blighted. They lost most of the cattle and had to sell off the rest for less than a dollar a head.

Instead of giving up on the ranch, they both decided he would go East again and organize a cattle drive from Texas to California. A five-dollar Texas steer would bring up to one hundred dollars in the California mining towns. That would give them enough money to buy another starter herd.

It would be a hard and dangerous drive across Apache country and deserts, swollen rivers, and mountains. But it would be good money if a man made it.

It had been hard to leave Louise, the hardest thing he had ever done in his life. But her strength and her insistence made it easier. It was when he reached Fort Worth that he heard the news. Louise was dead. The telegram said it was cholera. An epidemic had hit Montrose, the town where she was staying until he returned.

He was almost destroyed by the news. He wandered down through Texas and into Mexico, hiring on as a ranch hand and on a couple of trail drives. He spent two lonely winters in desolate line shacks in the remote foothills of the New Mexico Rockies working to keep herds from scattering and to keep them alive in the blizzards.

By the end of the second winter, Seth knew he could not forget Louise by trying to lose himself or by trying to shut himself off from people. He knew what was happening. He knew he feared returning to their land. He was afraid he could not stand the pain of seeing it again.

Finally during that last winter he knew he would have to return. He would have to stand at her grave and say good-bye. She was buried as she had requested on the hillside above the site for their home.

It would be painful, but he would have to do it. He would have to try to carry on with their dream. It was that resolution that had brought him to the campsite on Sandstone Creek the night before. He was on his way home. He was on his way to exorcise a haunting memory.

The laughter from Chelsey's Saloon jolted Seth out of his thoughts as he walked by the open double doors. On impulse he decided to go in. It would be good to be around some people right then. A beer would taste good, too.

He entered and stood inside the doorway for a minute to let his eyes adjust to the dim light. The long wooden bar running along the left wall supported half a dozen ranch hands escaping the afternoon heat. A series of dusty mirrors multiplied the rows of glasses and bottles behind the beefy, red-faced bartender in a white shirt with bright yellow sleeve garters. The rest of the room contained tables and chairs for card playing and drinking.

He walked to the bar and ordered a beer. His gaze wandered across the room. A quiet poker game was in progress nearby. Then he saw Kirby sitting at a back table leaning over a glass and watching him.

Seth turned back to the bar and sipped his beer. He felt Kirby's stare at his back. In a moment he felt someone beside him. He heard Kirby's low, hoarse voice.

"So it's the man with the smart mouth." Seth ignored him and took another gulp of his beer.

"I want to hear what you know, March." Kirby raised his voice above a whisper now. The bartender watched them from a safe distance. The chatter at the poker table stopped.

Seth turned and looked at Kirby. The man's eyes were empty of warmth and of feeling. His mouth was a tight, thin line. Seth remained silent. He drained his glass and held it up to signal the bartender for another.

When Seth turned away from Kirby toward the bartender, he sensed his mistake immediately. He quickly looked back at Kirby, but it was too late. The man's fist already was in motion and there was nothing to do now but take the blow. It came hard into his stomach just below the breastbone. He gasped for air.

"I just wanted your attention, March. Now I'll teach you some manners."

Seth was bent over trying to breathe. It was a reflex he knew he should have resisted. The next blow would be a knee into the face or a fist on the back of the neck.

Quickly Seth sprang forward and butted Kirby with his head, shoving him backward over a poker table. Kirby hit the floor and began scrambling to get up. Seth inhaled deeply and stepped toward him. Kirby saw him coming and reached for his gun.

Seth swung his leg hard and aimed the toe of his boot at Kirby's jaw. Seth felt the solid impact and heard something snap. Kirby lay still.

"That man's gonna have trouble eating for a few days," said one of the poker players and went back to the game.

"You don't fight fair, do you, mister," the bartender said, grinning.

"You're wrong," Seth replied, picking up his hat. "A fair fight is one that's over before somebody gets killed." He headed for the door. "Sorry about the mess."

He tried not to wince at the dull ache high in his stomach.

CHAPTER 5

SETH had little choice. He would have to cooperate with the women even if their story about the bank robbery sounded farfetched to him. Their threats to accuse him of being the gang leader might be a bluff, but he couldn't take a chance. They were desperate.

Also, because of the fight Kirby would be more dangerous now. Seth couldn't leave the women to the bounty hunter's mercy. Marshal Brenner now was in no condition to protect them from Kirby. Next time Kirby wouldn't back down from Brenner.

There was no other way. Seth would have to help the women escape, give them the money, and be on his way. After that, he couldn't be responsible for anyone but himself.

He had learned many things in his thirty years. Breaking people out of jails was not one of them. He would have to figure it out as he went along.

First, he needed more information. That meant another visit with Brenner. Seth went by Doc McKinney's office. The doctor already had removed the bullet and patched up Brenner. The marshal had insisted on returning to his office, since he had prisoners in the jail room. McKinney shook his head as he told Seth, "He's a cantankerous old fool. But this town probably wouldn't be here if it hadn't been for Earl.

"He was the town's first marshal. Only one we've ever had. Been at it for more than twenty years now, hauling drunks off the street, getting shot at, getting hit now and then."

The doctor looked up at Seth. "You saved his life out there today, son. If you're going to be around Black Springs for a few days, we all would be much obliged if you'd keep an eye on him, at least until he gets his shooting arm well again."

Seth hated to hear that kind of talk. It made what he had to do a whole lot tougher. "I'm glad I could be of help, Doc. But I'm just passing through. He seems like a man who can take care of himself."

Seth then headed for the marshal's office. He admired Brenner for his courage. It took guts to try to take the drunk kid alive instead of shooting him. Although Seth didn't like the idea of helping the women escape from Brenner's jail, he liked even less the idea of getting himself arrested for robbery.

He could salve his conscience a little by reminding himself about Kirby. If the women were out of jail, Brenner wouldn't have to confront Kirby again, this time without a chance.

Seth found Brenner sitting at his desk with his right arm in a sling and trying to roll a smoke with his left hand. His face was pale and he was in pain.

"Come in, March," Brenner said. "We didn't get to finish our conversation. That little interruption out in the street may have put my shooting arm temporarily out of commission, but it'll really be serious if it means I have to give up smoking."

Tobacco spilled over the desk as Brenner's left hand fumbled the curl of paper. Seth reached over and picked up the paper and the tobacco sack and began rolling a cigarette.

"Thanks for the fast gun out there," Brenner continued.

"Some of the folks told me you're about the fastest they've seen in a while."

Seth ran his tongue along the edge of the paper, rolled it over the tobacco, and gave the end a twist. He handed the smoke to Brenner.

"I'm sorry it had to come to killing," Seth said. "The kid didn't leave me much choice."

"To tell you the truth, March, fast guns make me nervous." Brenner struck a match along the edge of the desk and lit the cigarette. "Unless, of course, the fast gun is on my side." He peered at Seth through the smoke.

"I'm a rancher, Marshal, not a gunfighter or a lawman."

"That's too bad. I could use a man like you. Well, anyway, watch out for Kirby. He's a mean one."

Seth nodded. "We just had a brief conversation over at the saloon. He'll probably be even meaner next time we meet."

"You'll meet again, all right," Brenner said. "I have to ask you to stay in town for a day or two. Kirby's prowling around and the Tucson bank is raising hell. I need to end this case as soon as possible, so I've wired the circuit judge. He's coming in for a hearing, and I need you to testify about your meeting with the women out at the creek. The hearing will be tomorrow about three o'clock."

"Hey, Marshal Brenner." A woman's voice came from the back room. Brenner leaned forward to stand but sat back again with a groan of pain.

"Seth, would you see what they want?"

Seth looked into the cell room. "Ladies, what can I do for you?"

Elizabeth smiled when she saw it was Seth. "Would you tell the marshal we need some drinking water?"

He turned to Brenner, who gestured toward a pitcher of water and two tin cups. Seth carried them back to the cells. "Here you are, ladies. It's not my wonderful campfire cof-

fee, but it's wet." He filled the cups and handed them
through the bars.

"So, Mr. March, you're still in town?" Elizabeth said
with a smug smile.

"Still here, Miss Castle. Looks like they need me for your
hearing." He refilled the cups as the women passed them
around.

"That hearing should be some party." Elizabeth chose
her words carefully. "We girls wouldn't want you to miss it."

He returned the smile now. "I think I know what you
mean." He needed to let them know that he'd decided to
cooperate. "I'll just tell 'em what I told Brenner earlier. We
traded horses and you couldn't stay for coffee. That's about
it."

Elizabeth handed back the cups and nodded. "That's
about it, all right." Her green eyes were not piercing now,
he noticed. They were much calmer. She was counting on
him.

He walked back into Brenner's office and set down the
pitcher and cups. He couldn't look at Brenner. Seth wanted
this whole troublesome business over.

He stepped out onto the boardwalk. Two men dressed in
suits and white shirts were looking at the marshal's broken
window and talking in low voices.

Seth had to have a plan to get the women out. And he
didn't want to make Brenner look bad. Maybe it could take
place when Brenner was out of the office. But if a bullet
wound wouldn't keep him away from his job, then what
would?

The two men walked on down the street. Suddenly Seth
realized what he had overheard them say. He opened Brenner's door and stuck his head in.

"Marshal, is it true about a reward? Ten thousand for the
return of the money?"

"I'm afraid it's true. The Tucson bank sent a telegram this

morning. I've been trying to keep it quiet to avoid a mob scene. It could be worse than a gold rush around here."

"Thanks, Marshal," Seth said. "I won't tell a soul."

He closed the door and walked to the edge of the porch. He leaned against the porch post, thrust his hands deep into his pockets, and stared at the ground. So the marshal feared a mob scene. He looked down the street at the townsfolk coming and going. A few ranch hands were leaving the saloon.

Seth smiled. He had the escape plan. He wished he could go right in and tell Elizabeth.

Elizabeth sat on the bunk and leaned back against the wall and wondered about Seth March. Should she trust him? What choice did she have? He would have to come through. And if he didn't? Well, she knew she would never accuse him of being part of a robbery. Yet the threat of tying him into the robbery was the only weapon she had.

A jury in Black Springs probably would think her story unbelievable. Back in Tucson the jury probably would believe the story because they knew Alfred Pound and the way he ran his bank. But Pound had so much power in Tucson that no jury or judge there could be trusted.

So she had to trust Seth March, just as she had trusted Alfred Pound once.

Except for Alfred Pound, she had enjoyed Tucson and her job there as a schoolteacher. She smiled at the thought of her school class seeing her now in this jail cell. This jail room and the marshal's office were about the size of her one-room school, the Sydney J. Pound Public School of Tucson named for none other than Alfred Pound's father.

Alfred tried to demonstrate his generosity and public spirit by providing the land and funds for the building, but only if the city council would name it after his father. The council was so happy about the donation that they conveniently overlooked the fact that Sydney had been a drunk and a bum until he swindled his prospector partner out of a silver-mine claim.

After that, Sydney no longer was a drunk and a bum. He was just a drunk, and a wealthy one. When he died, his son Alfred began trying to buy him respectability. The city council was happy to cooperate.

Elizabeth looked through the bars at Frances in the next cell. Frances was just a year or two older than some of her students had been. All of them had been young and eager and fresh and full of life. Elizabeth had taught them for only one year, but it had been a happy year.

Elizabeth always had wanted to be a teacher. While growing up she was taught at home by her parents. They both were teachers in Memphis, Tennessee. Then the yellow-fever epidemic of the seventies hit Memphis.

She went to live with her grandfather in St. Louis. She never saw her parents again. They died of the disease a few months after she had left. She had been ten years old.

Her grandfather had promised her parents he would rear her and see to it that she got an education. So, when she was sixteen, she went to Alice Winthrop Burroughs Teachers' College for Women, a fancy girls' school in St. Louis. The school's founder, Alice Winthrop Burroughs, was convinced that women could civilize an unruly world if they were refined and educated in the classics and the social graces.

At the college Elizabeth acquired not only a good education and a knowledge of refined society but also a disgust of hypocrisy and refined society. She much preferred her grandfather's bar. His name was Patrick McMullin and she and half of St. Louis called him Patty. She loved him very much.

Patty was a bartender and an Irish tenor and sang with a quartet at the bar in the evenings. They were wonderful. He gave her a love for music.

Someone was speaking to her. It was Lou, with her face pressed between the bars. "I asked you, 'What are you smiling about?' "

"Oh, I was just daydreaming about my grandfather," Elizabeth said. She thought for a moment more. "He used to say to me after he had sung all evening and into the night, 'Liz, my girl, ye must have the best book learnin' we can afford. That I promised right happily to your parents. But aye, Lizzie, don't forget the ballads of Ireland. All the learnin' in the world won't make your heart glad like a wee bit of Irish singin'.' "

Lou nodded. "Your grandfather was right, Liz, and you've inherited his taste for blarney, too."

Elizabeth laughed. "I hope the judge tomorrow doesn't think I have a touch of blarney."

She looked down the row of cells at Lou and Frances, Kate and Rosa. Elizabeth shouldn't have involved them in all this mess. They had come along out of loyalty. She couldn't let them be punished for her actions. They didn't owe her a thing. She had hired them for her show and she had protected them from the saloon customers, who mistook them for bawdy-house girls. They had repaid her by making the Gray Lady Theater in Tucson a success. They also had been her friends through some tough times.

She stood and walked to the bars separating her cell from the next. "Lou, I think you girls should go on to San Francisco without me. I'm the only one the bank wants. Then as soon as I clear this up, I'll join you. It should be only a few days."

She smiled and tried to appear unconcerned. The others were listening. From the expressions on their faces she knew she hadn't turned in one of her most convincing performances.

Lou answered solemnly. "Liz, we know you're worried. It was your money and you had a right to it. But when you pull a gun in a bank and lock people in a vault, well, that's trouble."

"We know you're trying to keep us out of trouble," Rosa said from two cells away, "but Kate and I've been talking, and we think you stand a better chance if we are all tried together."

"That's right," said Frances. "A jury of men might be willing to convict a redhead, but how many men would be able to refuse a blonde?" Frances playfully pulled her yellow hair across her face and winked at Lou.

"And two blondes guarantee acquittal," said Lou, striking a dramatic stage pose.

Elizabeth laughed. "What do you two know? Maybe the judge stays up nights thinking about redheads." She knew that beneath the clowning the others sensed the seriousness of the charges, yet they were sticking with her. To get these loyal friends out of the mess she had made of things, she would have to do it against their will.

"Liz, listen!" Lou said abruptly. "I think I hear Seth March talking to the marshal."

Sure enough, Elizabeth heard Seth's voice, then the sound of the outer door being shut. Marshal Brenner entered the cell room. He moved slowly and stiffly, trying to keep his arm from swinging.

This was the first time she had seen Brenner since the shooting. The sight of the injured marshal filled her with apprehension, for herself and for the girls.

Maybe her anxiety was because of Seth. She had heard he had shot the gunman. Did that put him in danger? She pushed that thought from her mind. They needed him to help them. Beyond that she should have no concern for him. She returned her attention to the marshal.

He was holding out a book to her with a yellow ribbon tied around it. "Here's the book you wanted to borrow. March just brought it by. He said he'd give it to you as a present."

She stifled her surprise and took the book. "Thanks, Marshal. It gets boring in here with nothing to do."

"It's kind of strange," Brenner said as he walked back toward the office. "Didn't figure March as a man who'd be reading books." He paused in the doorway and looked back. "Also, I don't know why he'd want to do a favor for somebody who gave him the short end of a horse swap."

He looked at the young women for a moment longer and chuckled. "Then again, maybe I do know why a man would be inclined to do you a favor."

When the sheriff was in his office, Elizabeth looked at the book in her hands. It was *The Iliad* by Homer. She had read some of the Greek classics in school. But it surprised her to see this book out here, especially coming from a drifter like Seth March.

Quickly she pulled off the yellow ribbon and opened the book. Something heavy dropped out and she grabbed for it. It bounded off her hand, against her dress, and hit the floor. There at her feet lay a derringer like the one she had used at the bank.

She stepped forward to hide it under her skirt. The others had seen it, too. They all waited, hardly breathing. Maybe Brenner had heard and would come back to check.

She looked in the book. The center of the pages had been cut out and the derringer had been placed in the hollow like an egg in a nest.

She was surprised by her feelings. This book with its heart cut out could mean their escape, yet she felt a touch of disappointment. She liked books and had wanted to read this one as soon as she saw it. At the same time, she was delighted by Seth's ingenuity and by this sure sign that he had a plan of some sort. The smuggled gun also put him at odds with the law. He now was involved in a criminal way and would have to see it through.

Apparently the sound of the dropped pistol had not alerted the marshal. She stepped back and picked up the pistol. Only then did she notice the piece of paper rolled up in the barrel. She slipped out the paper and put the gun under her mattress.

She turned to the wall and unrolled the paper. It was a note printed neatly in pencil. "At hearing tomorrow tell them you hid money near pool where they caught you. Make it sound convincing."

She passed the note to the others. There was something about Seth's instructions that bothered her. If she told them she had hidden the money, that would mean confessing she had taken it. Also, Seth wanted her story to be convincing. Not many people would believe she had stolen her own money.

Well, no matter, it was the truth. And the truth was what she'd tell, at least until she got to the part about hiding the money.

She picked up the book from the bunk where she had pitched it. Maybe a few pages of reading remained uncut. On the inside cover in a woman's handwriting appeared the faded words "To Seth from your ma and pa."

A wave of nostalgia swept over Elizabeth. She felt sad. She thought of her own parents and the books they had given her. And she was puzzled. Why would Seth travel with a book like this unless he were reading it? And what must have gone through his mind as he cut out the heart of a book that must have at least sentimental value for him?

Well, Marshal, it appears Seth March is a reading man after all. And he's probably much more he doesn't appear to be, too.

CHAPTER 6

WHEN Seth reached the edge of town he pointed his Appaloosa west. He had been relieved to see Brenner take the book back to Elizabeth without any questions. Seth had tied the ribbon around it to discourage the marshal from looking inside. It had worked.

He had hated cutting the pages to get the derringer in it. But it was the best way to avoid suspicion. The book was one of his favorites. He remembered the Christmas when his mother gave it to him.

She had taught him to read. He probably would have learned to read with the Bible, the way she had learned to read, except that his father was staunchly against religion. His father, named Joshua from the Bible, had been beaten severely while growing up every time he committed what his own father, a Methodist minister, called a "sin against God." Those sins included even small mistakes, like forgetting to wash up for supper.

By the time Joshua turned sixteen he finally had had his fill. Then he committed the ultimate sin: He struck his father. In fact, he hit him several times in a brawl between the two that had been a long time coming. The son held his own against the father, kissed his mother good-bye with bruised lips, and never saw his parents again.

About the only thing he took with him and never lost was a hatred for religion. So Joshua's own son, Seth, grew up on the Greek classics. The minister's son didn't suspect that they were about religion, too. Those old stories consoled Seth the way the Bible consoled others. The stories of Homer taught him about truth and about life, and they gave him lessons for right living the same as the Bible.

For years Seth had carried the two books by Homer in his saddlebags. They were important to him, especially during those long winters in the line shack after Louise died. That's when he read them through time after time.

He wondered now why he had been willing to destroy one because of Elizabeth. Was she becoming that important to him?

He knew his decision had something to do with his struggle to let go of the past. It almost had killed him during the three years after Louise had died. He was just beginning to learn that lesson from the Greek stories. A person has to give up the past, whether a dead wife or a treasured book, in order to have a future. Maybe sacrificing that book his mother gave him would buy him a future, just as heading back to California to say good-bye to Louise in her grave would allow him to go on with his dream without her.

Those questions would have to be answered another day. He was approaching the railroad tracks now. He had work to do.

He rode up the tracks until he came to the top of a rise. It would be steep enough to slow the train to a crawl. About a half mile south of the tracks stood a grove of scrub oak that would provide good cover for the wagon.

He rode back down the tracks for about three miles and began searching for something to block the rails. In a nearby gulch he found a dead juniper that had been washed out of the ground. He threw a loop around the trunk and dragged the tree to the tracks. Now all was ready for the next day.

It was getting dark as he rode back into Black Springs and

headed for the stable. It had been a long day since that wagonload of women had interrupted his breakfast that morning. He deserved a hotel bed for the night.

The next morning he took his time over breakfast. There was no need to rush. The hearing wasn't until three o'clock. He felt comfortable and confident in spite of the trouble he had wandered into. Part of the reason was because of that hotel bed he had just gotten out of.

In the past three years he had slept in a regular bed only about a dozen times. The ground with a saddle for a pillow is okay until a man tries a bed again. Now he knew he was spoiled for at least a month.

He figured he had another reason for comfort. There were people in his life again. That gave him a future. Even if it were only a one-day future, he had that to plan for and look forward to.

His first stop was at the train station. He started to ask for six tickets to Maricopa. He realized at the last second that six might create suspicion, so he asked for three. He would come back later for the rest.

Next, he headed for the stable to buy a team and a rig and to borrow a horse for the afternoon. He picked out two horses from the corral, and Jake helped him hitch the team to the wagon. Then Jake went back to his work at the forge.

There was no communication about the shooting the day before or about the drunk who wanted to kill a Papago. But when their eyes met, Seth knew that Jake had not forgotten.

He admired Jake. He was a craftsman who knew his trade and did it with pride. But Seth sensed something tragic in Jake's manner. It was more than just his silence that made him seem tragic. It seemed he had a kind of secret wisdom, the kind gained from suffering.

Seth thought of the story in Greek legend about Proteus, an old prophet who had the ability to change his shape to that of any creature he desired. If a man could hold onto him until he changed back to his original form as a man, Proteus would answer any question asked of him.

In that story there was a man named Menelaus, who had fought in a war for ten years and was trying to find his way back to his home and his wife. He was able to capture and hold onto Proteus even though the old man changed into all sorts of fierce creatures. The question Menelaus finally asked was simply, "How do I get home?"

That was what Jake seemed like to Seth. Jake seemed like someone who had the answers but would remain silent until you saw him the way he really was.

The question Seth would ask would be the same as Menelaus' "How do I get home?" How does a man get back to that home he thought he had years ago and then lost? Where is it now? How does a man return to it?

He had learned to laugh at himself when he had thought such as these. He knew they came from his book reading, and he knew they made him see the world a little differently from other people. He never talked about his stories to anybody. Most people wouldn't understand what he saw in them. But then most people hadn't grown up with the stories or lived with those heroes for two lonely winters in a line shack.

He left the livery stable and drove the wagon out to the scrub oak grove he had spotted the day before. He trailed his Appaloosa behind along with the borrowed horse. He left the wagon hidden on the side of the grove away from the railroad tracks and hobbled the two wagon horses and his Appaloosa in a grassy hollow just beyond the trees.

Then Seth rode back down the tracks on Jake's horse until he came to the dead juniper he had dragged there the day before. He pulled it across the tracks.

The next train would be coming out of Black Springs at

six-thirty heading west. It was the run that the five women
had arrived on two days earlier. If all went well, they
would be on it again that evening.

He arrived early at the schoolhouse where the hearing
was to be held. Now he had six train tickets in his pocket.
Just as he had hoped, the station agent had been out in the
afternoon and someone else had sold him the other three
tickets.

Promptly at three o'clock the judge arrived in a black,
one-horse buggy. Elizabeth and the other women soon followed in their rig, with Marshal Brenner riding just behind
them. He must have wanted the rig there in case it was
needed as evidence. That suited Seth's plan well. It would
save him from having to hitch up the team later.

The judge was old, thin, and slightly stooped. He walked
with a cane and wore a black broadcloth suit. His cheeks
were sunken and he puckered his lips before he spoke a
word of greeting to the townspeople he knew.

The people addressed him as Judge McBain. He carried a
heavy, leather-covered Bible, and he looked to Seth more
like a preacher than a judge.

Seth was pleased to see that the schoolroom was filling
fast, with some men standing in the back. This case had
created interest not only because the suspects were women,
but also because news of the ten-thousand-dollar reward
had spread quickly through the town and back to the
ranches scattered up and down the valley.

Just as Seth expected, Roscoe Kirby was there. Kirby had
an ugly, puffed-up bruise on the right side of his jaw. He
stared at Seth for a moment and then looked away sullenly.

The judge sat at the teacher's desk on a raised platform.
He pulled a pistol out of his coat pocket and placed it on the
desk beside the Bible. The five women were seated along the

front bench, with Brenner at one end and a small man in a gray suit at the other end. Seth remembered that the man had ridden with the posse through his camp.

Judge McBain banged the desk with the butt of his pistol, pursed his lips, and said with a clear, firm voice, "Quiet down, folks, and let's get started."

The crowd fell silent.

"This is just a hearing and that's why we don't have a jury or any bothersome procedures like that. I'm going to try to find out what happened, and if it looks like a crime has been committed, we're gonna have us a trial."

Seth had no idea if this was the proper way to go about having a hearing. Probably no one else in the room knew either. Most people in this territory figured a judge could handle these matters just as he saw fit so long as it seemed reasonably fair.

McBain looked at the row of women. "Now, you ladies know you can have an attorney here to represent you if you think you need one."

Elizabeth nodded and said, "Your Honor, we're sure you'll see right away when we tell our story that we're innocent. So we really don't need a lawyer."

The judge gazed at Elizabeth for a moment. He looked bored. He had heard it before. Then he turned to Brenner. "Marshal Brenner, tell us why these women are in your custody."

Brenner stood and pulled a chair up beside the desk and sat facing the audience. "Early yesterday morning I was given a telegram saying that the Tucson Cattlemen's Bank had been robbed of fifty thousand dollars. It said that a woman named Elizabeth Castle had done it and that she was heading west on the train with four other women. It said they might be getting off anywhere along the way and to watch for them.

"Well, Judge, some folks had seen these women arrive the night before and told me they were staying at Borden's Hotel. By the time I got there they were already gone and had been seen heading south on the wagon road.

"I rounded up a small posse, including Tommy Myers there, who was opening up Cavanaugh's General Store about then." The small man at the end of the bench proudly lifted his chin.

"The women had about a thirty-minute head start on us, but we made up most of that by the time we crossed Sandstone Creek. There was a fellow named Seth March camped there. I sent the posse on ahead while March told me the women had swapped horses with him."

"Is that man in the room, Marshal?" the judge interrupted.

Brenner looked about the room and spotted Seth. "He's standing there at the back, Judge."

Seth gave a friendly wave. "I'm Seth March, Your Honor."

"Mr. March, when the women came through your camp, did you know they were being pursued by the law?"

"No, Your Honor, I just knew they were in a big hurry. They wouldn't even stay for a cup of coffee." A few people chuckled.

"Did they tell you why they were in a hurry?"

"Yes, Judge. They said they were Mormons fleeing persecution." Quiet laughter spread through the room.

McBain quieted the room with a stern expression and turned back to Brenner. "Continue your story, Marshal."

"By the time I reached the posse they already had caught up with the women."

"Marshal, when you arrived were the women resisting arrest or otherwise acting like criminals?"

"Well, no, they weren't exactly acting like criminals."

"What exactly, then, were they doing?"

Brenner hesitated, and then said in a low voice, "They were taking a bath."

The crowd broke into laughter. The judge began banging on the desk with his pistol. "Let's have order now. Crime is no laughing matter." He puckered his lips while he waited for silence.

Seth leaned back against the wall and smiled broadly. This bit of news made him admire the women all the more.

Judge McBain urged Brenner to go ahead with the story. Brenner told about being tricked when Elizabeth pulled the rifle on them and that soon she surrendered. He told about searching the stream and the surrounding area for the money and finding nothing.

Now it was Elizabeth's turn. Seth found himself nervous for her. A murmur of whispering arose as she stepped up and sat in the chair beside the desk. The crowd was mostly men, and they were shifting around and craning their necks to get a better look at her.

Seth knew they were seeing what he saw that first morning. She had fixed herself up for the trial. Her red hair was put on top of her head, giving her a respectable, prim and proper look. But it also made her look even more beautiful.

The judge was patronizing and treated her like a child. "Miss Castle, now you tell us what happened and how you came to be charged with bank robbery. Just take your time. These are pretty serious charges. We want to hear your side of it."

Elizabeth sat upright in the chair and stroked her hair lightly. Seth sensed immediately that she would be capable of a convincing performance. She smiled sweetly at the judge and began.

"Your Honor, I'll have to begin back in Tucson about six months ago if that's all right."

The judge nodded and spoke softly to her. "Just take all the time you want, young lady."

"About six months ago I was part owner of the Gray Lady Saloon and Theater in Tucson. My partner, Skid Wiggins, ran the bar and the gaming tables in the saloon, and I was in charge of the stage shows in the theater next door."

McBain frowned at this news. "I know, Judge, this doesn't sound like a respectable endeavor for a lady, but the Gray Lady was a respectable place, and our entertainment included the finest in song and dance. These ladies sitting before you performed at the Gray Lady nightly, and they can testify that it was first-class place." Lou, Kate, Rosa, and Frances all nodded solemnly.

Seth knew this was the start of a good show. He thought Elizabeth might be inventive, but this was beyond his expectations.

"Well, one night, as I said, it was about six months ago, my partner died suddenly." Elizabeth gazed at the floor sorrowfully. Seth figured she was trying to work up a tear or two.

"What did he die of, Miss Castle?" McBain asked sympathetically.

"It seems, Judge, he died of what in Tucson would be regarded as natural causes."

"What was that?" the judge pressed her.

"Well . . . uh . . . he died of bullet wounds during a poker game." The crowd broke into loud laughter again.

Judge McBain pounded the desk angrily, his face turning red. Seth laughed with the others around him. He saw even Marshal Brenner's shoulders shaking with laughter. The effect Elizabeth previously had had on the judge was gone now. He didn't like looking foolish.

"Miss Castle, this is serious business here and we'll not have this hearing turned into another of your stage entertainments."

Elizabeth showed innocent surprise. "Your Honor, I beg your pardon. I wasn't trying to be entertaining. I just didn't know how to put it. It was a grievous loss for us all." The other four women nodded in unison again.

"Go on," said McBain, scowling.

"Well, since Mr. Wiggins had no living heirs, a judge in Tucson decided that the saloon should be mine, since I was his partner. Also, he decided that Mr. Wiggins' winnings in the poker game at the time of his . . . uh . . . demise should be mine, too.

"Now, since Mr. Wiggins died in one of those back-room, high-stakes games, there was considerable money involved. And there seemed to be some controversy as to whether Skid Wiggins deserved to be winning. That was what the shooting was all about."

McBain cleared his throat. "Are you suggesting your partner might have been cheating, Miss Castle?"

"Oh, no, Judge. That's just the point. There was no evidence whatsoever of cheating in the game. That's why the judge at the hearing said that I was entitled to the winnings that lay on the table in front of Skid when he was shot. Of course, that didn't include the money in the pot that was being bet at the time of the shooting."

She had caught McBain's curiosity about the law. He couldn't resist asking, "What was the judge's decision about that money, Miss Castle?"

"Well, Your Honor, the judge just couldn't decide who should have the pot. Skid held the winning cards, and everybody knew it. That's probably why he got shot. But the hand never was finished. The judge couldn't decide.

"You see," she explained, "Skid usually made those decisions about games in the Gray Lady. But he was dead and the judge never played much poker." McBain smiled along with the audience.

"So," Elizabeth continued, "the pot finally was given to

the Methodist Church for a new building." Even Judge Mc-Bain chuckled this time along with the laughter and only halfheartedly rapped the desk for silence.

Seth was enjoying the performance so much he almost forgot the seriousness of the hearing. Elizabeth might win them over with her imaginative story, but could she convince them about hiding the money? He began to wonder if she wasn't taking a big chance with such a yarn.

"So you found yourself a wealthy woman with a saloon to run?" McBain asked. He seemed to be enjoying the story, too.

"Yes," she said, "but I learned soon enough that I couldn't manage without Skid and there was no one else I thought reliable enough to handle the job. I knew I would have to sell the Gray Lady.

"Besides, I had hired four other girls as singers and dancers to give the Gray Lady the best stage show between St. Louis and San Francisco. I wanted to take them on a performing tour to other cities.

"That's our first love, Judge, performing onstage and helping people forget their sorrows."

McBain puckered his lips and nodded slowly. "I'm beginning to see that, Miss Castle."

She continued, "So I sold the saloon and deposited the money where I had already put Skid's poker winnings, in the Tucson Cattlemen's Bank."

The crowd stirred a bit, trying to make the connection with the robbery before she told them. Seth was beginning to wonder himself how she was going to pull it all together.

"That was probably one of the biggest mistakes in my life. I had paid little attention to the fact that Alfred Pound, the president of the bank, also had been in that poker game and had been the biggest loser. Mr. Pound was not known as a good loser, Your Honor.

"Well, on Monday afternoon, the day before yesterday,

the girls and I were leaving Tucson for San Francisco, where we were to perform for six weeks at the Pacific Theater. I went to the bank to arrange to have the money transferred to San Francisco.

"It was then that Mr. Pound told me I couldn't have my money. He said his lawyer was going back to court the next day to get the judge to change his mind about giving me the poker-game winnings.

"Mr. Pound just grinned at me and said, 'I'm sorry, Miss Castle, but it seems that new evidence has been uncovered. A witness will testify that Wiggins was cheating.'"

Elizabeth leaned toward McBain for emphasis. "Your Honor, I couldn't help saying to Mr. Pound, 'Is that the same witness who testified that Skid Wiggins drew first, even though Wiggins never carried a gun and everyone knew it? And isn't that so-called witness also the foreman who runs your ranch south of Tucson?'"

Seth believed that if Alfred Pound had entered the room right then the crowd would have hissed and booed. Elizabeth had convinced them that she was an innocent victim and Pound was a black-hearted villain.

"Then Mr. Pound became furious and ordered me out of his bank. He said I'd never get the money. I told him that even if the court allowed him to hold the money, that order wouldn't be good until the next day. I still had a right to my money until then.

"Mr. Pound just laughed and said, 'You don't have any rights in my town, lady.' Well, before I knew it I was pointing my derringer at him and telling him to bring me the fifty thousand. Then I locked him up in the vault with his employees and jumped on the train and got off at Black Springs and here I am."

Seth smiled at the scattered applause. He promised himself he would try to catch her act in San Francisco if they all got out of this mess.

Elizabeth then told of her chase across the valley in the buckboard and of the encounter with the posse at the pool. Now came the part Seth was waiting for.

"What about the money, Miss Castle?" McBain asked.

"I really hate to tell, Judge, because the money is mine and we had hoped to go back to get it. But, since I believe in telling the truth, here goes." She paused for dramatic effect. "We hid the money near the pond before the posse arrived."

"But the posse looked, Miss Castle. Marshal Brenner testified about that already."

"But the posse was looking for a large sack of money. We couldn't find a place to hide something that large, and we didn't have time or tools to dig a hole. So we each took an armload of the money and stuffed it down gopher and rabbit holes all around and in the hollows of trees and under fallen logs."

Elizabeth must have guessed the reasons for Seth's instructions. She was creating exactly the right effect. Seth noticed a man near him nudge his neighbor and whisper something to him. Then they both quickly slipped through the doorway.

Seth smiled at Elizabeth as she watched them leave and then glanced at him.

She knew what was happening, all right. She poured it on now. "Each bundle had about a hundred bills in it. Some were bundles of ten-dollar bills and some were bundles of twenty-dollar bills. Also there were several one-hundred-dollar bundles. I guess altogether we hid about forty or fifty bundles all over that area near the pool.

Three men were working their way toward the door from the front of the room, and Seth noticed one man who had been sitting at the window drop out of sight outside it.

Judge McBain began watching the crowd stirring about as Elizabeth droned on. "I think I hid most of my bundles under logs that I could roll over quickly. But when I heard the posse, I quickly tossed my last bundle of hundred-dollar bills into some rocks beside the falls."

By this time half the men in the room were on their feet, pushing and shoving to get out. Most were crawling over the four windowsills because the doorway was jammed with bodies.

A man who had fallen to the floor was being trampled and began to curse loudly. Outside, the school playground was becoming a bedlam of horses and shouts.

Marshal Brenner was on his feet, surveying the situation nervously. Judge McBain's calls for order were lost in the noisy confusion.

Elizabeth sat waiting innocently and smiled slightly at Seth, who smiled back broadly. He then had to duck a swinging fist that caught a neighbor in the back of the head.

"Damn it," the angry fighter was shouting, "all I want is one bundle! Let me out of here!"

Seth couldn't see Kirby anywhere. He must have gone to try to protect the bank's property. Seth made his way to the front of the room.

Brenner was leaning over the desk and shouting to Mc-Bain, "Can we have a recess until tomorrow? I'm going to have to get out there to that pool before these boys start killing each other!" The judge nodded and continued sitting stunned and silent at the desk.

Brenner called Tommy Meyers over and began making arrangements for him to take the women back to the jail and to stay with them.

This was Seth's chance. Checking to see that McBain was completely distracted, he leaned over and whispered to Elizabeth, "Wonderful performance. Make your break when you hear the six-o'clock train whistle. I'll be on the street with a rig." He didn't have time to say more. Brenner was turning toward them.

"March, aren't you riding on this wild-goose chase?" Brenner eyed him with suspicion.

"No, Marshal. And I'd guess you wouldn't either if you didn't have to. It'll be worse out there than going barefoot at a rattlesnake hunt. I'll tell Doc McKinney to expect some busted noses and a few broken bones."

"I'm afraid you're right." Brenner turned to Elizabeth. "I'm not sure what your game is, ma'am, but you sure play it well."

Seth stood in the schoolhouse doorway and watched Brenner ride out of town to the south and Myers proudly drive the women back to jail in the rig. Seth looked back into the schoolroom. Judge McBain still sat quietly staring into space. He noticed Seth, pursed his lips, and shrugged his shoulders. Seth responded with a shrug and slowly walked toward his horse.

McBain would be okay. He might even decide one day that this hearing was the highlight of his legal career. It was about the best show Seth had ever seen.

Seth had little to do until the Central Pacific westbound blew its whistle at six o'clock. Then he'd have his hands full.

CHAPTER 7

THE town had settled down when Seth rode over to the jail and offered to take the rig back to the livery stable. He wanted to be sure it would be ready to use later.

At the marshal's office Tommy Myers was pacing back and forth along the boardwalk, looking serious, and carrying a rifle. He had also pinned on a deputy's badge and strapped on a pistol. He still didn't look much like a lawman.

When Seth made his offer to take care of the rig and team, Myers quickly agreed. He was enjoying his sense of self-importance too much to bother with chores like stabling horses.

Seth drove the rig over to Jake's. The blacksmith wasn't anywhere in sight. Seth walked into the stable next to the blacksmith shop. It contained two rows of stalls and smelled of fresh hay and manure. At the back of the room beyond the stalls was a door to what probably was the tack room. That probably was where Jake slept.

Seth headed toward that door, then heard footsteps behind him. Just as he turned, a gun barrel was jammed into his ribs. Someone lifted Seth's pistol out of its holster and then backed off. Two men were silhouetted against the light at the stable doorway. Seth couldn't make them out.

"To the tack room, cowboy. Let's go."

The small tack room smelled of leather from the harnesses

and bridles lining the walls. A small, dirty window cast a square of sunlight on the floor.

Seth looked at the two men entering behind him. He knew immediately who they were. These two also rode with the posse that brought the women in. Both men were about average height, but one was wiry, with a very narrow face. The other was stocky and bore the marks of a fighter. His crooked nose hadn't healed right, and a scar ran above his left eye.

Neither man had shaved for three or four days. They were dressed as ranch hands in homespun pants and cotton shirts and both wore battered, wide-brimmed hats. The thin one wore a rattlesnake hatband.

"Sit down, ladies' man. We want to hear you talk." Crooked Nose gestured with his gun toward the narrow bed. Seth sat down. It was the only piece of furniture except for a small table and a trunk against the opposite wall.

"March, we've got a little problem and we think you can help. We know the lady told a phony story at the hearin' 'cause me and Walter was out there with the posse and we went all over that creek area the redhead was talkin' about. We didn't find nothin' that looked like money."

Walter, the thin-faced one, sat on the trunk and kept his pistol pointed at Seth. "That's right, mister, and we did some thinkin'. We reckon you're the only one who could have hid that money. Now, some fools are gonna go out there and stick their hands down gopher holes and get bit. But Luke and me, we aim to get the reward money."

Luke sneered. "We are law-abidin', you see, ridin' on the posse and all. And we're gonna turn you in unless you talk to us about that money."

Seth figured they were only guessing. "You heard my story at the schoolhouse, boys. If I knew where that money was, do you think I'd still be in Black Springs?"

Walter snorted a laugh. "You might wait around, March. You just might if you had four or five lady friends to spring out of jail. I'd wait for a day or two myself on a couple of those fillies."

"Here's the deal, March." Luke seemed confident he had a sure thing. "You tell us where that money is hid, and we let you ride free as soon as we find it. But you play it stupid and don't tell us, and we blow your head off." Luke pulled back the hammer on the .44.

Seth just shrugged. "You kill me and what have you got?" He still was pretty sure they were bluffing.

"What you don't understand, March, is that we know you plan to bust those women out while everybody is out there at the creek goin' loco," Luke said.

"Maybe we ought to tell him everythin', Luke," Walter added. "He seems to be kind of slow at catchin' on."

Luke put his boot on the bed and leaned toward Seth. "You see, March, it's like this. Walter here has got a sister who works down at the train station. Sometimes she sells tickets when the agent's out of the office." Luke turned to Walter. "I think he's gonna catch on this time."

Luke continued, "When you bought three tickets this afternoon, Walter was there visitin' his sister and saw you from the back room. Well, Walter got real suspicious 'cause he remembered seein' you somewheres before."

Luke paused to let it soak in. "Walter has a real good memory, March. He might not look like much but he's got a real good memory." Walter's smile spread across his thin face.

"Walter did some checkin' when the agent got back and, sure enough, you had bought three tickets before. Now, me and Walter didn't have much schoolin', but we can count to six. And we figure you're plannin' a little trip this evenin' with some fine-lookin' company.

"Maybe you might gamble your own life," Luke went on,

"but you're not goin' to let those fillies down when they're dependin' on you. I just know you're not."

Seth forced himself to smile and leaned back casually against the wall. He had been stupid to buy the tickets.

"Well, boys, I guess you got it figured out, all right. But we're gonna have to make a deal before I talk about hiding places. I'm not riding out empty-handed."

His only chance was to get them to relax and then go for one of the guns. If he named a hiding place, they would either take him along or tie him up, check it out, and come back for him. Either way, he wouldn't be able to get the women to the train by six o'clock. And either way, it wouldn't be pleasant when they learned he had lied.

"We might let you have a little travelin' money," Luke said. "How much do you think he'd take to ride off and leave those ladies, Walter?" Walter looked at Luke and chuckled.

That was Seth's chance. He kicked out at Walter's gun hand and saw the pistol fly, then lunged forward at Luke. As Seth's left fist plunged into the stout man's stomach, Seth turned to deal with Walter. But Seth couldn't turn completely. Luke had grabbed his left arm.

Seth raised his right arm to block the blow he knew would come from Walter. A dull pain shot across Seth's skull and down his neck. Blackness closed in.

It sounded like a train whistle in the far distance. It was faint and fuzzy, like a dream. He felt sick to his stomach. His head throbbed. The light from the window made him shut his eyes in pain. The train whistled again. He tried to make sense of things. He sat up slowly.

It came back suddenly. He had to get the rig over to the jail. The women would be coming out soon with no way of escaping.

The two men were gone. Seth didn't have time to figure it out. He felt his way out of the tack room and walked groggily through the stable. He realized now he had been hearing the clank and ring of the anvil since he had come to.

He walked out into the late-afternoon light and tried to blink away the bright pain. He was relieved to see the buckboard where he had left it. It still was hitched to the team. He rounded the corner and looked into the blacksmith shop.

Jake was at the forge. He smiled when he saw Seth standing in the doorway holding his head. Jake pointed with his hammer at the opposite wall. Luke and Walter were sitting on the dirt floor bound hand and foot.

"You're a lucky man, March," Luke said angrily. "Chief No-Speak here busted up our party. But as soon as you make your break, your Injun friend will find out what kind of trouble he's in."

Seth knew that Luke was right. If he went through with the jail break, Jake could catch hell. Luke and Walter could claim they were trying to bring Seth in. But Seth had to go through with it. Elizabeth might already have made the break. They might already be waiting for him. Brenner seemed to be a fair man. He would realize that the Indian couldn't have known about the escape.

There was no time to explain to Jake. What explanation could Seth give, anyway? A simple thanks was not enough.

Seth doubled his fist, thumped his chest once, and held his open hand toward Jake. Seth hoped it meant thanks of some sort. Jake smiled and turned back to his work.

Seth glanced about the street as he drove the team to the marshal's office. The men had not returned from the creek yet. The town seemed to be quiet.

The marshal's office was just ahead. Seth hoped all had gone well inside and that Elizabeth and the others would be ready. The train was in the station now. Only about five minutes had passed since he had first heard the train whistle back in the tack room.

* * *

At the first sound of the train whistle, Elizabeth was ready. "Okay, Lou, that's your cue," she said. Then Elizabeth clutched the derringer to her stomach and bent over, groaning.

"Mr. Myers!" Lou screamed frantically. "Mr. Myers, come in here quick! Liz is sick! She must have gotten food poisoning from that slop you fed us!"

Myers raced into the cell room looking frightened. He fumbled about trying to put the key in the lock. When Elizabeth heard the squeak of the iron door swinging open, she stood up and pointed the derringer at Myers' chest.

He stood starring at the pistol. His face turned ashen. "Liz, I think you'd better let the deputy sit down," Frances said. "He's going to faint dead away."

"Okay, Mr. Myers, take a seat. But as quickly as you can, take off your clothes," Elizabeth ordered.

That snapped him out of his fear. He looked at her. "That's what I said, Mr. Myers. The clothes must come off. You're only slightly larger than I am and I need your clothes."

Myers obediently began to peel off his shirt. His face changed from pale to scarlet.

"It's only fair, Mr. Myers," Kate called from two cells away. "You made us put on our clothes yesterday. We make you take off yours today." The deflated clerk starred at the floor silently. He continued undressing.

Elizabeth felt sorry for him. "You're a brave man, Myers. The marshal will know you had to do it." She tied him up with a lariat she found in the marshal's office and tied a handkerchief gag around his mouth. She quickly slipped out of her dress and into his white shirt and gray trousers and jacket. They almost fit. Then she took Myers' key and locked him in her cell. "Okay, Elizabeth, now get us out of here," Lou said impatiently. "We should be able to find better accommodations than this."

Elizabeth found it tough to speak now, but she knew she must not appear uncertain. "All right, girls, Mr. Myers, I want everybody to get this straight. I'm getting out of here and I'm going alone. That money's mine and I don't have to share it with anybody. If you girls were sucker enough to let me play you along for cover, well, that's your own doing."

She saw the surprised looks on the girls' faces. They hadn't known about this part. She looked to see that Myers was listening.

"I took this money from the bank by myself and I'm solely responsible for it. You hear that, Mr. Myers? Tell it to the marshal. These girls had nothing to do with this bank business. I just strung them along. Maybe they're stupid but they're not bank robbers."

She looked directly at the women. "Also, they don't have any idea where that money is. I took care of that myself, too."

"Elizabeth, you can't do this," Lou said. The look of surprise had become one of disappointment now. Elizabeth felt sick about leaving them. She hoped they soon would see that this was their best chance for release. And five women on the run were too easy to spot.

Elizabeth spoke with a quiet, sad voice. "You girls have a show or two to do in 'Frisco. You'll be okay." She wanted to cry. She wanted to give them all a hug and tell them she loved them and would miss them. But she knew she couldn't. Her role wouldn't allow it. She was playing the tough bank robber who didn't care about these suckers she had taken advantage of. Another moment and she might have weakened, but just then she heard a rig pull up outside.

"Thanks for the clothes, Deputy. You're welcome to my dress if you get chilly." As she ran out of the room she heard them calling her name.

Tearfully she grabbed a derby off the hat rack at the door and pulled the derby on her head. She stuffed her hair up under it and looked out the window. Seth was waiting with the rig.

Seth glanced about nervously. Few people were on the street. Would he have to go into the office? Maybe the women had trouble. At that moment, the door opened and a small man came dashing out. His hat was pulled down low. He grabbed the edge of the buckboard seat and started to swing up.

"Wait a second, mister, I . . ."

"Hello, partner." Elizabeth looked up at him, smiling from under the black derby two sizes too big.

He laughed and helped her up. "You are a surprising woman, Miss Castle."

"If you'll call me Elizabeth, I'll call you Seth, and maybe we can get out of here. This is a jailbreak, you know."

He drove toward the station, and she explained about the girls and the deputy's clothes. "Oh, by the way," she said, "this probably will look better on you." She reached over and pinned the deputy's badge on his shirt.

"There you are, Seth. Now you're officially escorting a prisoner."

He grinned. "Right. And we have six official tickets." They were passing the saloon when two drunk cowpunchers tried to cross the street in front of them. He suddenly pulled the team to a halt.

"Hey, boys," he called to them, "want to take a train ride to Maricopa? They've got a casino up there like you've never seen before. It's a free trip up. You get back on your own."

The two drunk drovers looked at each other. "Harvey," said the larger one, "have we ever been drunk in Maricopa before?"

The other considered the question seriously. "Well, Matt, I wouldn't remember that, but I know we've never been sober in Maricopa."

Matt looked up at Seth. "I guess that settles it. We're going to sober up in Maricopa." They climbed into the back of the buckboard, falling over each other and laughing. As the rig pulled away, two more punchers stumbled out of the saloon.

"Hey, Stump, Buster, come on!" Harvey shouted. "We're going to get sober in Maricopa." The two ran, stumbled, and cursed as they caught the rig and were dragged aboard by their companions.

"That's better," Seth said. "Now I'm a respectable deputy with five prisoners again. It's much better cover for us. Besides, I couldn't take this deputy job seriously if I were only guarding a little man with a hat pulled over his eyes."

He and Elizabeth were treating this trip like a picnic. It was much more serious than they were pretending. But he was in a festive mood and so was she. As long as they did what they had to do, why not enjoy it as long as they could? There could be tough days ahead.

At the station he waved six tickets at the conductor and they boarded the train.

"They're all wanted back in Maricopa," he said to the conductor. "We may be of some annoyance to the other passengers." The drunks had begun to sing loudly. "Any chance we could have this car to ourselves?"

The conductor looked about. "I think we can arrange that. Seems like we're not too full this evening." He went up to move a few passengers to the next car.

Seth sat beside Elizabeth while the cowboys sprawled out in the back. He breathed a little easier as the train chugged out of Black Springs.

CHAPTER 8

THE train had an uphill pull to Maricopa. The rugged country was a mixture of rocky gorges, flat ranges, and low ridges. Desert basins began a few miles to the south and stretched on into Mexico. High country began rising to mountains in the east and the west. Not far from the tracks the Santa Cruz River ran down the center of the valley.

It was rugged country, but a man could run cattle here. Seth's thoughts wandered to the land waiting for him in California. But he wasn't ready to go there just yet.

He glanced over at Elizabeth looking out the window. She was a remarkable woman. He had seen her in action out on Sandstone Creek and in the hearing, and he had just seen her make a jailbreak. In all of that, he had spoken only a few words to her.

"Elizabeth, I want to congratulate you on that story you told about the bank robbery. I've heard some yarns before, but that one topped them all."

Elizabeth frowned at him. "Seth March, you mean you still don't believe me? I'm both insulted and flattered. Insulted because that means you think I'm really a thief and a lying one at that. But flattered because you must think I'm good at it."

"Are you telling me that all that business about Alfred Pound is true? The fifty thousand really is your own money?"

"If you don't believe me by now, Deputy, it won't do much good to answer that question."

Seth had to think this over. What if the story were true? He had seen her do some unusual things. And she certainly didn't fit the mold of a thief. Yet she already had proven she could be a convincing liar with that tale about hiding the money. He just didn't know what to think of her.

The train began to slow. They would be coming to the tree he had dragged across the tracks.

"By the way," Elizabeth said, "what do we do now? It just shows you how much I trust you. I don't even know our plans."

"As soon as the train stops, I help them drag the tree off the tracks. Then we go on a ways."

"How do you know there's a tree on the . . ." Elizabeth stopped talking and smiled. "I specialize in bank robberies and you specialize in escapes. We ought to consider taking up this vocation full-time."

The train came to a halt to the sound of hissing steam. "Just sit tight," he said. "I'll be back in a minute."

The conductor met him at the steps. "You look like a man who can handle that gun you're carrying. We may need your help."

"What can I do for you?"

"A tree's been dragged across the tracks and it could be an ambush." The conductor glanced about. "Some Apache burned out a ranch north of Maricopa last week, and we spotted a hunting party of Papagos near here a couple of days ago."

He followed the conductor to the front of the train and kept a lookout. Four men dragged the tree off the tracks. He hadn't counted on Indians. He knew the Apache still were raiding to the north and east. But he didn't know they had moved this far south. And he knew very little about the Papagos.

He returned to the passenger car and sat down beside
Elizabeth. The four other "prisoners" had started a poker
game in the back of the car. The train began moving.

"We'll get off about five miles ahead," he said. Elizabeth
nodded silently.

A few minutes later the train began to slow again as it
climbed the steep ridge Seth had noticed the day before.

"Okay, Elizabeth. Let's just ease on out to the landing for
a breath of air."

He leaned out from the steps and looked down the tracks.
The locomotive almost had topped the rise. They were
moving about the speed of a man running.

The wheels clicked loudly against the rails directly beneath them. "This is where we get off!" he shouted. "I'll go
first. When you step off, hold onto me and hit the ground
running."

He swung down and managed to keep his feet on the loose
cinders along the roadbed. He kept running as he reached
up for Elizabeth. She hesitated for a moment and then
jumped.

He caught her around the waist and then stumbled over a
crosstie. They went down, tumbling to the bottom of the
embankment. He felt the cinders biting into his hands as he
tried to break the fall. His left knee banged into a rock. The
clickety-clack of the train quickly grew fainter, and soon
they were left in silence.

He got up quickly to see if Elizabeth were hurt. She had
lost her derby, and her coat was torn. She sat up, dusted
herself off, and looked at him.

"That was some exit we just made," she said. It was good
to hear her laugh.

"Sorry," he said and helped her up. "Any broken bones?"

"Nothing broken. Just a few bruises and a mouthful of
dirt."

They began to look about. The sun's rays were slanting

over the ridge, casting a shadow on most of the basin before them. There was over an hour of daylight left. The evening coolness had not yet come to relieve the day's heat.

Elizabeth looked puzzled. He saw her concern. It appeared they were miles from anywhere and no transportation was in sight.

He smiled. "How about a short evening stroll?"

He led her across the basin about a hundred yards to the scrub oak grove. As they came through to the other side, she saw the wagon and two of the hobbled horses grazing in the basin beyond.

"Aren't you clever!" she shouted and turned and threw her arms around his neck.

He was paralyzed by the pressure of her warm body and those green eyes looking into his. Just as quickly she backed away. Her move surprised and embarrassed them both.

Awkwardly, he tried to carry on the conversation. "I guess I wasn't clever enough to plan for what comes next. But I think we'd better do some traveling while we still have daylight."

They walked toward the wagon. "I left provisions out here for five people, two horses for the wagon, and a mount for me. As I recall, the deal was that I'd help you escape, tell you where you could pick up the money, and then I'd head west. But now that you're alone, I can't just leave you here."

"Don't do anything you don't want to do, Seth. I can take care of myself."

He had no doubts about that. But still it didn't seem right to him. Also, he wasn't so sure anymore he wanted to ride off alone.

"We can't figure that out now," he said. "Probably Brenner won't get back to town till dusk and won't lead out a posse till daybreak. But we can't take the chance they won't come tonight."

Seth also had Kirby on his mind, but he didn't want to worry her about that yet.

"Let's ride till dusk. We can head up into those hills toward Table Top Mountain southwest of here. Even if a posse comes this evening, those footprints and the hoofprints I left yesterday where the train stopped for the tree should slow them down till dark.

"You sort through this gear and grub. Pick out what we'll need and can carry on horseback for the next few days. We'll leave the wagon and one horse here. I'll be back as soon as I round up our mounts."

He took a bridle and a halter and set off down the slope. He caught up his Appaloosa and got the buckskin for Elizabeth. He saw no sign of the third horse, a pinto. Leading the buckskin, he road bareback over the ridge. He couldn't spend much time looking for the horse, but it'd be cruel to leave the animal hobbled. He wouldn't last long with coyotes running in packs.

From the ridge he spotted an arroyo at the far edge of the basin. He rode over and saw the pinto at the bottom at a small spring. He removed the hobble and gave the horse a slap on the rump.

Back at the wagon, he put the only saddle he had brought on Elizabeth's buckskin. He would ride with just a blanket on his horse. They filled the saddlebags and he rolled the rest of the gear in blankets and tied it behind the saddle.

With Seth leading the way, they galloped the horses along the ridge and southwest toward Table Top Mountain.

Elizabeth watched Seth's broad back move rhythmically with his horse's gallop. She knew very little about this man, yet she trusted him enough to follow him up into the hills alone. She couldn't figure him out.

Obviously he was a cowpuncher, but not just a hand for hire. And he read books. There was that book he had sent her in jail, and then another book she found when she was packing the saddlebags. She would have to tread softly. He seemed to be a man who was reluctant to reveal much about himself.

She had been relieved he hadn't deserted her at the wagon. She had said she was capable of taking care of herself, but she really wasn't so sure about that. She didn't know this country, and there still was a reward out for her.

She had not wanted him to be obligated to take care of her. If he helped her, she wanted him to want to help.

After they left the river basin they began to ride through especially arid country. Mescal stalks rose here and there among the scrub oak and mesquite. They were gradually climbing toward the barren hills of Table Top.

At sundown they stopped and made camp near a small spring in a ravine. Already she was sore from riding and was glad to stop. She was not accustomed to sitting in a saddle. She knew there was much more to come and she was determined not to complain.

They decided they could risk a fire, since it was almost dark. Seth left her to fix the bacon and beans in the single skillet while he watered the horses at the spring and filled the canteens.

She busied herself with supper and found she was in a surprisingly good mood. The setting sun filled the sky with reds and oranges, and the crackle of the fire was cheerful. The smell of the bacon reminded her of mornings long ago when she was a small girl. Troubles lay behind and ahead, but it was pleasant here.

Seth tethered the horses nearby and dragged two rocks up to the fire for them to sit on. They ate supper out of tin plates and talked about possible plans.

She could see that Seth was eager to head on to California. He didn't say exactly what it was that was pulling him west, but it seemed to be an obsession with him. Nevertheless, he seemed willing to see her through this crisis.

Back in Black Springs he had been motivated by her threat to accuse him of being in on the bank job. She felt bad now about having to use that threat on him. But it seemed he wasn't helping her now because of threats. Was he a natural gentleman who helped his neighbor? Or was it something else?

"There are two things I want to do now," she said in answer to his question about plans. "I want to go back to get the money. Then I want to head for San Francisco. The girls should be there soon."

"Okay, we should be able to manage that." Seth looked at her for a moment. "For what it's worth, I was thinking about your story on the ride up here. I think you're telling the truth about the bank. Seems to me you have a right to that money. The Alfred Pounds of the world have to be beaten now and then. I don't want him to get that money back. I'll help you all I can." He smiled. "My only regret is that I wasn't in that bank when you locked him in the vault."

"You would have loved it," she said. "He was so angry his face was the color of that sunset. Even though I was scared to death, I still enjoyed it."

"I hid the money back at the campsite by Sandstone Creek. When we get it, we'll have a drink to your victory over Alfred Pound." Seth lifted his coffee cup in a toast.

"Now," he continued, "how do we get back to the money?" He thought for a moment. "When the marshal in Maricopa gets the wire about the escape and talks to the conductor, he'll hear about the tree across the tracks and about the four drunk prisoners who arrived without the deputy escort.

"He'll tell that news to Brenner, and Brenner and the

posse and the bounty hunters probably will figure we got off where the train stopped. They'll figure we're circling back southeast toward Black Springs or toward the creek for the money, since we didn't carry anything with us on the train.

"They might figure we've already headed out of the territory. Either way, if we stay in these hills for a couple of days before heading back east to Sandstone Creek, we probably can avoid a posse."

She liked the plan. She also liked the fact that he believed her and wanted to prevent Pound from getting the money. There was a certain decency about this cowpuncher. After they recovered the money she would hate to see him ride off.

It was dark now. Seth threw a few more sticks on the fire and dropped another handful of ground coffee into the pot. The stars were coming out directly overhead and the fire crackled warmly. They sipped coffee in silence for several minutes.

She was exhausted, but she wasn't ready to sleep just yet. The events of the past few days since she walked into the Tucson Cattlemen's Bank had been the most exciting of her life. She wouldn't ever have planned such days as these. It all would have seemed too dangerous or difficult. But now that it had happened, it was thrilling. She wanted to savor it all while it still was fresh.

Seth stirred the fire, then broke the comfortable silence. "Elizabeth, I'd like to ask a favor of you. I'd like to hear some more of your story. Everything I've heard you tell so far would put the finest trail-drive storytellers to shame. Tell me some more.

"For instance," he continued, "there's still part of your story I can't fit together. How did you ever end up part owner of a saloon?"

She laughed. "How I got into that situation is just as hard to believe as what you know already."

"I kind of figured it would be, coming from you." Seth poured her some more coffee. "But you go ahead. I believe everything you say now."

"Okay, here's your story. I became part owner of a saloon because I always wanted to be a schoolteacher."

"I should have guessed it'd be something like that." He laughed. "Okay, let me have it."

"I was brought up by my grandfather, Patrick McMullin, and graduated from teacher's college when I was about twenty. But I got a happier education in Patty's bar than in that refined college. That bar was almost always filled with good humor and music."

She paused for a moment. "There were the other times, too. Sometimes Patty would think about his wife who died years earlier, or he'd think about my parents. Then he'd sing the sad ballads of Ireland, and you could hear tears in his voice. Some of the river men who also had seen hard times on the Mississippi said he sang those ballads the best.

" 'Lizzie,' he would say to me, 'an Irish song can fill your heart with life when sorrow has emptied it.' "

She grew silent for a moment, then looked up and noticed Seth was watching her carefully.

"I suppose," she said with a smile, "that's why I did what I did when I heard that Patty had died. He was killed when I was teaching school in Tucson. I had come West because I wanted to travel and explore. There were teaching jobs in St. Louis, but I wanted to go where the children really needed me.

"Patty had made the West sound golden. He called it the Land of Opportunity. I thought I would be escaping the snobbery and hypocrisy I had seen at Burroughs College. I learned soon enough that along with the honest, hard-working folks out here there are the hypocrites just like back East.

"During my first week in Tucson, I was told that I should

feel indebted to the man who had paid for the new school building. An old friend of ours, Seth."

"I think I already know."

"That's right, Alfred Pound had built the school and named it after his daddy, who certainly did not deserve the honor.

"During my second week at that school, Alfred himself came by and reminded me that I wouldn't have had that job if it hadn't been for him. Then he hinted that we should be close friends."

"But Patty had warned you about men like Pound?"

"Yes," she said, nodding, "I knew what the banker was leading up to. I was angry at his suggestions and his propositions, but I politely refused. He wouldn't take no for an answer. At first his offers were coated with promises of gifts and money. Then they came with threats of dismissal from the school.

"Finally, when I could stand it no longer, my refined Burroughs College manners gave way to McMullin bar manners. I told Pound what he could do with his proposal and with his school.

"I received my dismissal notice the next morning as I was packing to return to St. Louis. Pound had pulled some strings and convinced the school board of God-fearing parents and city fathers that I was a loose woman and not fit to teach innocent children.

"I really didn't care. I would miss the children, but I had already decided to leave. Then that same afternoon I received a telegram saying that Patty was dead. He had been shot trying to break up a fight in the bar.

"That news was so hard to take, I didn't know if I could stand it. I remembered Patty's advice about Irish ballads as a cure for sorrow and I longed to be back in his bar.

"In the rooming house where I lived, I could hear the

music and celebrating in the Gray Lady Saloon down the street. There I sat in my room with my bags packed and now with no place to go. I began to think that if I could just go down the street to that saloon and sit at the piano and play one ballad, then I would be closer to Patty again. It would be a kind of tribute to him, a way of saying good-bye, like a memorial service."

She noticed that Seth was listening with his head bowed. He seemed to be lost in thoughts of his own. No doubt he, too, had been in such a situation before. She wasn't sure if she should continue.

He looked up at her and smiled gently. "Please go on."

"Well, my memories of Patty drew me toward that saloon. But after I had left the rooming house I remembered that ladies in Tucson were not supposed to enter saloons. It wasn't considered proper.

"At that point I didn't care what Tucson society thought. Most of the people probably were convinced by Pound that I was a fallen women anyway. I decided to let them think what they wanted. There was more truth and purity in one of Patty's ballads than in all the social opinion in Tucson.

"I marched into the saloon and walked right up to the piano. I sat down, hardly noticed yet in the confusion of men drinking and smoking and talking and shouting. Then I began to play. I just wanted to play one Irish ballad in tribute to Patty and then I'd leave.

"I began to play 'That Irish Love of Mine,' one of his favorites, thinking all the while on Patrick McMullin and hearing his tenor voice lift pure and clean. About halfway through the song, I heard singing. I thought maybe I was just imagining it because I wanted so much to hear Patty again.

"When I turned from the piano, I realized that the crowd had become quiet except for three or four men who were singing along. They were dressed like railroad workers, and there was no question they were Irish.

"They raised their mugs of beer in my direction and kept on singing. So I kept on playing and sang with them, 'How I miss that Irish love of mine, I wonder where he roams. . . .' " Her voice lifted above the snap of the fire.

"By the end of the song about a dozen men had joined in, and I was playing and singing for all I was worth. Then they were shouting for more.

"I had planned for a one-song memorial service. But I remembered Patty always loved to sing far into the night. It seemed a more fitting service for him if we sang a while longer.

"The bartender had put a shot of whiskey down on the piano for me. I looked at the whiskey. I'd had only about two or three drinks in my life and those were only on special occasions. 'Oh, what the hell,' I said, and I raised the glass to the ceiling. 'Here's to you, Patrick McMullin,' I said in my best Irish brogue. 'You're the finest Irish tenor that ever my ears did have the good fortune to hear.'

"Then I downed the whiskey, gasped for air, and added, 'And you're a man who loved his whiskey.' And then I launched into a night of singing."

Seth was laughing now. She knew he was enjoying the story. Whatever had troubled him earlier now was forgotten.

"Skid Wiggins owned the place and offered me a job on the spot as a singer. I was a bit tipsy from the whiskey and I accepted.

"Over the next few months I brought in a lot of business. I wasn't that great, but the show was unusual—schoolteacher turned showgirl. Most of the time women in saloons are there for other purposes.

"Skid bought the general store next door and we turned it into a theater. He gave me a share of the business to make sure I'd stay." She laughed. "Over the next few months, every time I talked about leaving he'd give me another 5 or 10 percent ownership.

"We brought in the other girls—Lou and Kate and Frances and Rosa. Occasionally a traveling troupe of actors would come through and perform plays. We had pretty good entertainment in that old place."

She paused and stared into the fire, then continued in a lower tone. "Then Skid was killed in the poker game, and you know the rest." She was feeling a tightness in her throat again at the thoughts of Patty and Skid.

"Skid was a good-hearted man and an honest one. It's been said before, hasn't it? The good ones die young."

Seth looked at her quickly, as if she had read his mind somehow. Then he looked off in the distant darkness and remained silent.

She reached for the coffee pot. "Well, that's my story. What about you? I've talked enough. From the look on your face, maybe I've talked too much."

He looked at her and smiled. "No. I enjoyed your story. Thanks for telling it." He held out his cup for more coffee. "I figured you were from back East and had some education. I guess I also figured, or at least hoped, that you weren't a thief. You didn't seem greedy enough or desperate enough when you came riding through my camp."

"You mean you let us take your horse even though you weren't afraid of us?"

"Well, I was afraid you might shoot me, but not out of greed or desperation. I was afraid that you might pull the trigger because you were so nervous. Besides, the only way I'd get to know what five women were doing running from the law was to trade horses with you. I figured they'd catch you soon."

She laughed. "I think you're sneakier than I am. Also, you've changed the subject. What about your story?"

Seth stood up. "My story will have to wait. We should be getting some sleep. As I recall, Brenner likes to start his posse early in the morning."

Seth got the blankets and put hers on one side of the fire and his on the other. She sat quietly and watched. He lay down, said good night, and pulled down his battered hat over his eyes.

Elizabeth lay down too and watched the coals cool to a soft orange. She thought about something else Patty had said about singing the sad ballads. It shows that the grief you feel because your world ends can be the beginning of something good and true. "It's like a robin singing in the darkness just before the dawn, Lizzie," he had said.

Maybe sorrow in a roundabout way had brought her a new day. Seth seemed to have his darkness, too. She wondered what his dawn would bring.

CHAPTER 9

THE sunlight warmed Seth's face into wakefulness. He roused and was quickly alert. He had overslept. The sun was above the hills. He looked over at Elizabeth, still sleeping soundly.

He thought about her story the night before. She was a woman who had come to terms with her past. She had accepted her losses and had made the most of them. He envied her ability to tell her story with feeling and sorrow, but with good humor and no bitterness.

And when she had said, "Good night," he saw again that flicker of a smile and the hint of a laugh he had seen the first morning. They were haunting him.

He woke her and they packed hurriedly. He wanted to get deeper into the hills, where they would be tougher to find. The posse soon would see that they hadn't gotten off where the train stopped. And if they had a good tracker, they soon would be able to pick up their trail from the wagon, even though he and Elizabeth had walked across from the train tracks.

He still had not told her about Kirby. That would be one man who could find them. But Kirby probably would be able to figure out that they didn't have the money. Seth wondered again where Kirby went after the hearing. Surely he didn't believe the story Elizabeth told about hiding the bundles. Well, they would deal with Kirby when the time came. Right now they needed to make distance.

He gave Elizabeth some beef jerky to eat on their way and checked the canteens again. This was dry country. Even with the recent rains, springs like the one they were leaving were scarce. Later in the summer, water would be almost impossible to find.

"Okay, let's mount up," Seth said. Suddenly he stopped. She also heard it—the clapping of unshod hooves against the rocky ground. He suspected Apache.

They stood quietly for a few seconds. He guessed two horses, maybe three. If there were only a couple, maybe he and Elizabeth would have a chance.

He handed her the reins and climbed up to the rim of the ravine. The sound was coming from the other side of an outcrop of rock. He drew his gun and waited.

The clip-clop grew louder. Then from around the rocks a crusty old man on a mule rode into view. The man pulled up and drew a pistol as he looked about.

From behind Seth, the buckskin whinnied. The man swung the pistol in his direction. "Whoever's there, come on out!" the man shouted in a cracking voice. Seth motioned to Elizabeth to stay put and climbed up over the rim of the ravine. The old man looked harmless enough and Seth was relieved that they hadn't run into Indians.

The old fellow had a gray beard and wore a wool coat with several patches on it. He was sitting on a mangy mule and leading a second mule carrying a large load covered with canvas. A shovel was tied on top.

The man relaxed when he saw Seth and put away his gun. "I know you're wonderin' how I know'd you was there, young man. Well, I'll tell you. Gretel is never wrong." He gave the mule a pat on the neck. "Her ears start twitchin' whenever we get near people or varmints."

Seth motioned for Elizabeth to join them. The man slid off the mule.

"The name's Dusty Crane. This here's Gretel I'm ridin' and that there behind me's Jebediah. We've been together more years than I care to count."

Elizabeth led the horses up and stood beside Seth. "I reckon you two don't have to tell me who you are. I'd know'd you covered with mine dust at midnight. Them fellers were shore enough right. You are a looker, ma'am, beggin' your pardon."

Seth glanced over at Elizabeth, who wasn't sure what to make of the old man. "What fellows are you talking about, Dusty?" he asked.

"Oh, you folks are the talk of the countryside. I run into several punchers and prospectors in Black Springs last night. Some of 'em were laughin' about that little trick you pulled on 'em. The others was mad enough to bite off rattlesnake heads." He laughed and spat a stream of tobacco juice at a yucca plant.

"But both kinds were havin' themselves a good drink or two over it at the saloon. Some of 'em swear they haven't had so much fun since a herd of Texas Longhorns stampeded through town a few years ago.

"From hearin' them talk, that wild-goose chase must have turned into a brawl, and about half those boys ended up takin' a dunkin' in that crick. I'd-a given my best pick and shovel to a-seen that."

"You say you were in Black Springs last night?" Seth asked. "You make good time."

"Yep. Gretel here wakes me up before dawn and we're travelin' by first light. We're headin' over to the Colorado to hunt placer gold. Heard the stuff's all over the ground." He spat again.

"But I didn't expect to run into you two. Most folks

figured you was headin' on west with the money or down in
Mexico." He pulled on his beard. "I don't want to pry into
other folks' business, especially folks who can spin a good
yarn, but this must mean you ain't got the money yet."

Seth wasn't sure whether he trusted the old man. "I
reckon you're right. You don't want to pry into other
people's business."

The man laughed. "I don't aim to rile you none, young
man. But if I did want to pry a little, I'd tell you that you
don't want to stay in these hills right now."

Seth was curious and wished he hadn't spoken sharply to
the man. "What's in the hills that we won't like?"

"Well, as I said, there's a whole lot of folks lookin' for
you. Lots of people know about you now and some of 'em
have revenge on their minds and some are just plain greedy.
That little party yesterday just whetted their appetites.

"And to make matters worse, the reward was raised to
twenty thousand: ten for bringin' you folks in and ten for
returnin' the money. That banker feller must want you
caught real bad.

"Besides all that, they's got two posses after you. One was
gonna head out early this mornin' followin' the rail track,
and the other is headed by a couple of boys that got themselves tied up by the blacksmith. They was talkin' about
comin' up into these hills.

"Seems whenever anybody wants to hide for a while, they
hightail it up here. For some reason those two boys figure
you don't have the money and want to wait it out up here
until things cool off so you can go back for the loot.

"There was also this other feller in the saloon last night
askin' me if I'd run into you on my way into town. Mean-
lookin' maverick with part of his left ear missin'."

Dusty paused and thought a moment. "I saw a man once
before that looked that way. Got his ear bit off in a fight.
You want to stay shed of this *hombre*."

Seth realized now the prospector was right. They probably would be found if they stayed in these hills. Yet they would be spotted quickly and turned in if they left. The old-timer seemed to know the territory, and Seth needed more information. He suggested they have a bite to eat.

The sun was high in the sky by now and the day was heating up. They led the animals into the shade of the outcrop and sat down on a shelf of rock. Seth passed around the jerky, and Dusty offered them some biscuits from his saddlebags.

"Dusty, why are you telling us all these things?" Seth asked. "Why would you help people suspected of robbing a bank?"

The old man washed down the dry food with a swig from his canteen. "For one thing, I never had any money in a bank. And for another thing, it takes my kind of folks to come up with the story you told those boys, ma'am." He chuckled. "Shore wish I could have been at that hearin'." He shook his head and swore softly.

"And last, I know a little more than most folks around here about that there banker feller Alfred Pound. His pa and me did a little prospectin' about fifteen years ago. It never did amount to much. Sydney was a good man with the mules, wasn't much with a shovel. But then he started drinkin'. Well, we split up and he started prospectin' with ol' Pete Scarborough. Pete always dreamed of the big find.

"One day he and Sydney found it, found themselves some silver. Pete stayed back with the hole and Sydney went to file the claim. Only problem was, Sydney forgot real convenient-like to add Pete's name to the papers. Then he forgot to tell Pete about it till they had worked the claim for about a year.

"Pete got left with nothin', and Sydney got it all. Turns out there was not only silver but also copper, and Sydney got rich.

"Pete took it hard. You come across somethin' like that only once in your life if you're lucky. Pete got killed in a gunfight soon afterward. He never was no good with a gun. Got a gunfighter riled enough to draw on him.

"After that Sydney took more and more to drink until he wasn't good for nothin'. Finally drank hisself to death, and his boy Alfred ran the mine and bought that bank."

Dusty scratched his beard. "When I heard that story about ol' Alfred gettin' locked up, I downed a couple of whiskeys to you right there, ma'am. It's a fine thing you done.

"That's somethin' else I'd have given a mother lode to have seen." He laughed and slapped his knee. "Dadgum it, Gretel, we always miss the good ones."

"Dusty, I want to thank you for warning us about the posses. I think you might be of some more help to us. We're not ready just yet to head west."

Dusty smiled. "I reckoned you didn't have that money yet."

"You know these hills," Seth said. "Where can we go for a few days where we won't be found?"

Dusty grew serious. He looked at Elizabeth for a moment and then at Seth, sizing him up. He scratched his beard and pulled on his lip. "Well, mister, it's a mean choice you got. There is a way you can avoid these bounty hunters and the law, but I'm thinkin' you might prefer tanglin' with them instead of your other choice."

"If there's another way, we'd like to hear it," Elizabeth said. Dusty looked at her. He seemed to brighten when he heard her confident voice.

"I wouldn't suggest this, but it seems the lady has spunk, and you look like a man who can take care of hisself." Seth let him take his time. Whatever he was about to tell them wasn't going to be an easy solution.

"Seems to me nobody—no white man—would bother

you if you headed south for 'bout twenty miles." Dusty watched them to see if that made an impression. Seth figured he knew what was coming next.

"As you probably know, that's Papago country. Now, the Papagos haven't got a war goin' with the white man the way the Apache do. But the Papagos don't look kindly on white men or their cattle comin' down in their country. They're peaceful unless you come intrudin'.

"I don't hardly blame them none," Dusty continued. "We come in here stompin' around and takin' over their huntin' and grazin' lands. They see me prospectin' and leave me alone. Figure I don't take away what they need to live. But they don't have much use for the ranchers."

Seth thought about Jake. "Isn't the blacksmith in Black Springs a Papago, Dusty?"

The old man was sitting back on his heels now in the shade. "Well, I believe that's right." He looked up at Seth. "I heard you saved his life when some fool came to shoot him."

"I suppose I did," Seth said. "Jake gave me a sign of some kind. I think he was saying thank you."

"I heard he can't talk," Elizabeth said. "I heard he had his tongue cut out."

Dusty chuckled. "One thing I like about this country. You hear so many good stories. Fact is, most of the best ones are true." He thought for a moment. "Now, Jake's story is a good one, but I don't know if it's true or not."

He looked at Seth. "But about that sign. Is this it?" He pounded his chest with his fist and opened his palm.

Seth was surprised. "Yes, that's it. What does it mean?"

"I don't know exactly. But I've seen it before. A young Papago buck once gave me that sign. He was just a kid and his pony must of spooked and throwed him. It was down there in the Papago lands. I found him with his leg busted and he was almost dead. He had dragged hisself about three miles across the desert and had been bleedin' right smart. The turkey buzzards were circlin'.

"I patched him up best I could and then carried him on Jebediah to a Spanish mission about twenty-five. miles due south of here, and I left him.

"It was about a couple years later I was diggin' around a mesa. A whole passel of them Papagos come ridin' up madder 'n hornets. Seems I was on their burial grounds and disturbin' their ancestors or somethin'.

"Right then I had about as much chance of gettin' out of there alive as a gnat on a frog's nose. Then this buck I had helped steps up and looks hard at me. He gives me that chest-poundin' sign again. He says somethin' to the others and they mount up and ride off.

"Then before he goes he says somethin' else in a soft voice, with a lot of pointin'. I took it to mean I'd better get out of there and not come back or next time he couldn't save me.

"I'll tell you the truth. I'm not scared of many things, but I've stayed out of that territory since."

They had finished eating. Seth had a few more questions before the old-timer left. "Are you saying we stand a better chance if we head south for Papago country?"

"It just depends on what kind of chance you want to take. You have a better chance of not being put in jail again if you head south, but you might stand a better chance of stayin' alive if you hang around here. You might run into somethin' down there that would start you wishin' you could be in a nice, safe jail cell."

Dusty thought about the problem for a minute. "Maybe with the lady along, they'd figure you weren't there to stir up trouble. Just passin' through. You might make it.

"This would be about the right time to make your move. The posse followin' the railroad might have found where you cut up into the hills by now. They'll be comin' from the north. And that other bunch will be comin' up from the east. If you just head straight south you'd have 'em meetin' up with each other."

They all mounted up. "Thanks for your advice, Dusty. Hope you strike it rich soon," Seth said.

"I've about decided I get such a kick just watchin' people like you folks comin' and goin' and carryin' on so, I've got wealth enough in just bein' alive."

Dusty turned in his saddle. "Oh, one more thing: If you go into Papago country, don't try to hide from them. They'll know you're there. And if you talk to 'em, don't lie. They'll know that, too."

He started off. "Good luck to you. Shore wish I could have heard you tell that story at the hearin', ma'am." He disappeared into the ravine, cursing his mules.

Seth looked at Elizabeth. "How lucky do you feel today, partner?"

She looked back north and then east. "I've always wanted to see the desert this time of year."

They headed the horses southward down the rocky slope.

CHAPTER 10

BY midafternoon, Seth and Elizabeth had reached the edge of the open stretch of the desert basin. They rested the horses and surveyed the blistering, dry land before them.

"Might as well get on in there," Seth said. "We have water enough. If we camp here some bounty hunters might risk swinging this far south, especially if they picked up our tracks this morning."

They rode slowly into Papago territory. The desert contained arroyos here and there, and mesas always were in sight. Occasionally a small dune dotted with yucca plants rose from the flat desert floor. Saguaro cacti and scrub bushes stretched as far as they could see. There were plenty of places to hide. Seth could not tell if their feelings of being watched were just nervousness or if there were eyes following their movements.

Once he turned to check their back trail and thought he saw movement near a dune. It could have been a coyote.

They didn't talk much during the day's ride, partly because of a growing apprehension of what the day would bring. But there also was the mood that riding put him in. The rhythmic swaying of the horse was tiring after a few hours, to be sure, but it also put him in a daydreaming, thinking frame of mind.

He was surprised that Elizabeth could ride all day without complaining. It must be difficult for her. She had to be saddlesore by this time. But she always was willing to go on.

He wondered what drove her. She seldom spoke about the money. It had to be something else.

Late in the afternoon they stopped again to rest the horses. She looked tired. He said to her, "This trip has to be tough on you, Elizabeth. Why are you doing it?"

She smiled wearily. "It isn't just the money, and it isn't just anger at Alfred Pound." She thought for a moment. "I guess I'm searching for something. When Patty died, as I told you last night, it was difficult for me. I think I've learned to live with it, but it's left a big hole in my life. I'm not sure now what it all adds up to.

"I guess that means that an adventure like this is welcome. It might contain the answer." She grinned. "At least it fills the time until an answer comes along."

It sounded familiar to him—too familiar for him to want to think about now.

They rode on until just before dusk and then stopped to make camp. The day had been sizzling hot and they were exhausted. They were deep into Papago country now. They decided not to camp in an arroyo, where it might appear they were hiding, but made camp in the long shadows of a small dune.

Elizabeth knew she could keep the dangers of this country from her mind if she stayed busy. She helped Seth make supper. They found enough dead mesquite for a small fire. She knew she would not have ridden into this desert if Seth hadn't already proven himself to be reliable. He had handled every problem that had come their way so far.

She tried not to think about her soreness or about the heat and the dust from the ride. They could spare enough water only for her to rinse the dust and sweat from her face. That was so refreshing that it helped her forget the other discomforts of the day.

After supper the fire felt good against the cool of the desert night. She watched Seth feed the fire, and they sipped coffee as on the night before. She decided to try to draw him out a bit. She knew he, too, had a story to tell and seemed to want to tell it but couldn't.

"Seth, I've been wondering about your books. There was the one you used to smuggle the derringer to me in jail. I found another while packing the saddlebags back at the wagon. Do you always travel with a library?"

"Yes, but it's now half the size it was. That book seemed to be the safest way to get the gun to you. As you probably know, that book I cut up, *The Iliad*, was about a battle long ago that lasted ten years. And the one in the saddlebags is about the travels of a man named Odysseus after that battle."

He paused and thought. "I guess it's right that I cut up the one about the battle and that we still have the one about traveling."

"What are you doing reading these books? My parents had them when I was growing up, but nobody I knew ever read them. And at Burroughs College we weren't allowed to read them. We were told they contained too much violence, lacked morals, and were unfit for young ladies."

Seth laughed. "There is no more violence or immoral action in Homer's books than in the Bible, it seems to me. In fact, I was reared on these books the way some kids are reared on the Bible. My pa wouldn't have a Bible in the house and my ma wanted me to learn to read. So the Greek classics were what I read. It got so I would read them over and over and apply those stories to my life just as some people do with the Bible.

"Let me show you something." Seth reached over to the saddlebags and pulled out the book. He handed it to her. "Turn to page 159 and read the first paragraph on the page."

She opened the well-worn book and began flipping the pages. A picture fell out. She picked it up and glanced at it. It was a picture of a beautiful, delicate woman standing beside Seth. He wore a suit and looked dignified and uncomfortable.

Quickly Seth reached over and took the picture and put it in his vest pocket without looking at it. He turned and poked at the fire, embarrassed.

"I'm sorry, Seth. I didn't mean to pry." Then after a moment she said, "She's beautiful. Is that your wife?"

He glanced at Elizabeth and smiled faintly, "Yes. She's . . . her name was Louise and . . . she died about three years ago. I wasn't there. I was back in Texas trying to get a starter herd together and got a telegram about it after . . ."

She could see he was having a hard time but was trying to be polite and answer her question. "It's okay, Seth, if you don't want to talk about it."

"Well, it's just that I'm not used to talking about it. I'm just beginning to realize that I haven't really said good-bye to her. I've not visited her grave, even, and I think I have to do that before . . ." He stopped and took a deep breath.

"Let me tell you another story instead," he said. "Like I told you, some people have Bible stories that are important to them. This is an old Greek story from my reading that's important to me. You may have heard it before. It's about Orpheus and Eurydice."

She sat back and heard again the story she had read in her parents' home years ago. She always thought the story was a strange one.

"Orpheus was a musician," Seth began, "who could sing and play his harp so well that even the animals and the gods were charmed. Soon after he married Eurydice, she was bitten by a snake and she died. Her death was so painful for Orpheus he nearly died, too.

"Finally, when he could stand it no longer, he went down to the underworld, where everyone goes after death, to bring her back. In the underworld he sang so beautifully the gods promised that Eurydice could follow him back to the world of the living. However, Orpheus was warned that if he looked back at her before both of them were out of the underworld, she would not be able to return with him.

"When Orpheus entered the world of the living again, he could wait no longer. He turned to look at Eurydice. But it was too soon. She was not out of the underworld yet. She began to fade from his sight. He had lost her forever. His grief now was so great he wandered the earth in mourning until his death."

Seth was silent. Elizabeth knew that in this tale he had told her the story of the past few years of his own life. He must have loved Louise very much and he must have gone through a kind of hell, too, wanting her back. The old Greek stories did work for him as ways of telling about life and what people have to go through.

Seth cleared his throat. "I guess the looking-back part is the reason the story is important for me now. It doesn't bring them back to us, does it?"

He poked the fire again. "I remember a few lines from the story that make it seem like it was told for me." He thought for a moment. "Orpheus is speaking to the god who rules the world of the dead. It's a kind of poem:

I seek one who came to you too soon.
The bud was plucked before the flower bloomed.
I tried to bear my loss. I could not bear it.
Love was too strong a god."

Elizabeth wiped away a tear and couldn't speak. Seth finished his coffee as he continued to stare into the dying fire. Without another word, he stretched out his blankets near the fire.

A coyote howled a long distance away. The slight breeze was cool enough to cause Elizabeth to shiver. She rolled up in her blankets and watched the desert sky fill with a million stars.

CHAPTER 11

THE day already was stifling hot and it was only a couple of hours after sunrise. They had left at dawn so they could travel while it still was cool and then rest in the hottest part of the day. After another hour of riding they halted in the shade of a mesa. They unsaddled, staked the horses, and spread out the blankets for a nap.

Seth watched the strange beauty of the shimmering heat waves. The pressing heat reminded him that this was the kind of beauty that can kill. Without water a man might live two or three days here if he could stay still and had shade.

If he tried to travel, he had to know how to survive. First of all, he would have to be on foot. He couldn't keep a horse alive without water more than a day or two. The man himself could stay alive if he could keep his head and use what was around him. If the prickly pear or the saguaro were in bloom he could eat the fruit. It'd keep him from starving and also give him some moisture.

He also could chew on the pulp of the barrel cactus. And if it'd not been too long after the annual rains, he could dig down in the bottom of an arroyo and maybe find mud that he could strain through his bandanna.

Seth knew he wasn't going through this list just to exercise his mind. He knew what was happening. His survival instincts were being alerted now, as they usually were, by a threatening situation.

He had learned most of what he knew about survival from others, from the old-timers on the wagon trains and on the trail drives. And some things he had learned on his own, usually out of desperation.

The sad thing about learning to survive was that when he had learned the most and would be the best prepared to stay alive, he would be old. Then he would die just from being worn out. There was no way to prepare to survive that.

Without a doubt, death was on his mind. The heat waves, and the plants and animals that had learned to adapt in this desert, had put him in this mood. And, of course, his almost constant thoughts about Louise.

Elizabeth had fallen asleep, and he felt drowsy, too. Sleeping would be the best way to pass the hottest part of the day. He stretched out and watched a mescal stalk blur as he drifted off.

He awoke with a start. Elizabeth had screamed. Then he heard the dry, hollow staccato sound. Rattlesnake!

Elizabeth was standing motionless beside her blanket. She was hardly breathing. The rattler was coiled and vibrating its tail in the center of her blanket just two feet away from her.

Seth drew his pistol and fired. The snake's head jerked and the body began to writhe and twist in the sand. He carefully grabbed the tail and quickly flung the snake into the brush.

Elizabeth was terrified. She did not move. "Seth, it got me. It bit me on the leg."

She sat down and pulled up the trouser leg. Two bright points of blood marked the side of her calf.

He made her lie back and quickly pulled a rawhide leg tie off his holster. He tied it around her leg above the knee.

Then he raised her leg, shoved a stick inside the loop, and began to twist it tightly.

She moaned in pain and reached for the leg. "I know it hurts, Elizabeth, but it must be as tight as you can stand." He twisted it another half turn, and she clenched her fists. He let her leg down and the stick held in place against the ground.

He dropped to both knees and grasped her calf in both hands. Then he bent over and began to suck hard on the bite. He spit out blood, but he knew from the stinging-copper taste he was sucking out poison, too. He wanted to swallow. His mouth had been dry when he was awakened by her scream. He resisted the impulse.

He sucked again, hard, and this time left teeth marks on her leg. He couldn't be concerned about her pain. He sucked again and again, spitting each time. The calf was turning blue now, and the bite area was beginning to swell.

He opened the leather string for a few seconds. She didn't protest when he tightened it again, but clearly she was in agony. She began to ask for water.

He could do no more good by sucking and needed to wash out his mouth. He brought her a canteen and let her drink just a few swallows. Then he rinsed out his mouth.

Next, he fished around in the saddlebag until he found the chewing tobacco. He stuffed his jaw full and began chewing rapidly to soften it. He took a sip of water and continued chewing hard.

He was going through the motions now, almost without thinking. His mind was clear and alert. Instincts seemed to be taking over, giving orders, and his mind was working out ways to carry out the orders.

He gathered some sticks of mesquite and built a small fire. As soon as the wood was burning, he unsheathed his skinning knife and held it over the flames. The blade blackened and then the handle became almost too hot to hold.

Elizabeth had been watching, fear in her eyes. When he turned toward her with the knife, she lay back, closed her eyes, and covered her face with her hands.

He gave her the rawhide knife scabbard to bite on. Then carefully but quickly he made a short slash through the skin on each bite mark. The blood trickled down the smooth calf muscle and dripped onto the blanket.

The tobacco was soft and moist now. He took the plug out of his mouth and flattened it against the bite. A knot was beginning to rise around the wound, and the calf was continuing to swell. He wrapped his bandanna around her calf to hold the tobacco in place.

He released the rawhide again for a few seconds. While the leg was changing from blue to red, he cut the bottom of her trousers and ripped it up to the knee. Soon the leg would swell even more.

He tightened the rawhide again, this time fastening the stick inside her trouser leg. He still had much to do, but he wanted to make sure she was alert. She had hardly spoken since he had begun to work on her.

"Elizabeth, how are you doing?"

"I'm scared, Seth. It hurts and I'm scared. I don't want to die."

He was glad to hear her talk. Fear at least meant she was alert. Once he had seen a man go into a glassy-eyed stupor on the trail. The man was dead the next morning. But he also had seen men survive rattler bites because of sheer will to live. They'd get angry or scared or simply ornery and just refuse to die.

"I'm scared of dying, Seth. Be honest with me. What kind of chance do I have?" Her eyes were full of tears and pleading.

"Elizabeth, listen to me. I'm not going to let you die.

Please relax. You've got to stay completely relaxed and save your energy."

"Seth, if I die, promise me you'll not leave me out here. Don't bury me out here, Seth. It's just too lonely."

"Stop talking that way, Elizabeth."

"Just promise me that, Seth." Her eyes showed desperation and an absolute feeling of helplessness.

"I promise. I'll not leave you here."

She relaxed and closed her eyes. Tears were streaming down both sides of her face. Now and then he could hear her sob quietly.

The worst things working against them were the heat and lack of water. She needed to be in a cooler place. And she needed water. The times he had seen men survive rattler bites had been when they were given all the water they could drink.

And she was going to run up a fever. On top of the desert heat that might be too much.

If they had been in the hills or near water, he'd know what to do. But out here in this hell? And it would take days before she could ride; they had food and water for a few days only.

Maybe this was what the old prospector was talking about—not just the Papagos but other kinds of deaths in the desert as well. Maybe that's why he said they might be willing to trade what they would run into in the desert for a jail cell.

That old man surely had faced death a few times. That young Papago buck had saved his life at the burial grounds.

Suddenly Seth sensed that there was something important in the story he must remember. What was it? Dusty had saved the boy's life. Then he had taken him to . . .

That was it. Dusty had said something about taking the boy to a Spanish mission. He said it was about twenty-five miles due south of where they had been in the hills the day before. That would mean the mission, if there still was a mission, would be to the west, about four or five miles from where they were right then. They had ridden in a south-easterly direction about twenty to twenty-five miles from the hills. The mission could be an hour's ride away.

Was it worth the risk to try to get Elizabeth there? At a mission there would be food and water and a cooler place for her. There might even be a priest who would know something about doctoring.

However, to get there would mean getting her out in the heat, tiring her out, maybe killing her with the move. And they might not even be able to find the mission. Or they might find it and it would be abandoned.

"Seth," Elizabeth said. He bent over and rinsed her face with water. "Do something, Seth. It hurts. Please do something."

Her words were familiar to him somehow. Why did they seem haunting to him? He thought for a moment. Then he knew.

When he and Louise had lost the cattle to the drought, they discussed whether he should go to Texas to bring back a new herd. He didn't want to leave her.

She had said to him, "Seth, we must do something, or we lose our dream. If you have a dream and do nothing, then you have only a dream. But if you do something, anything, even if it's wrong, you have more than a dream. You have a life."

He still could hear Louise's voice. "Life is a series of struggles. If you don't struggle, where is your life? Go to Texas, Seth. That's all we can do if we want the ranch. Do something. To do nothing is to give up your life."

"Do something, Seth," Elizabeth said again. Her voice was growing weaker.

All right. He would do something. It might be wrong, but

he would do something. He wouldn't let her just lie there and die.

He would try to find the mission and he'd do it like the creatures of the desert. Somehow he would adapt as they did. The Papagos adapted. What would they do?

The answer came to him as soon as he asked the question. He took his knife and cut limbs from mesquite trees and lashed them together with strips of the blanket that he ripped apart.

By early afternoon he had made the crude drag he had seen Apaches use for their sick and their old. He hitched it to her horse and placed Elizabeth on it. He rigged up two poles over the drag and draped another blanket over them to make a canopy. It shaded the upper half of her body.

Her mind was becoming unclear now. She wasn't always sure who he was. She mumbled words he couldn't understand.

He pointed his horse due west and led her buckskin pulling the drag. It might mean her death. But it could mean her life. He could wait for the night or for the cooler evening, but he had no time. She might not last the rest of the day in the heat. And if he guessed right about the mission, they could be there in an hour or two.

It was a slow pace. He stopped about every fifteen minutes to loosen the rawhide and give her water. He also had to adjust the canopy and tighten the lashed poles. His frustration began to mount. He knew he wouldn't give up, but it began to occur to him more and more that his efforts probably were futile.

Elizabeth was unconscious and couldn't drink now. He could only bathe her face with water to keep her fever down when they stopped. She was burning. Her clothes were soaked with perspiration.

He had not paid much attention to what was happening

to him. Now he realized he was dizzy from lack of food and from working on the drag in the hottest time of the day. He had to remind himself to relax and stay calm. He would be of no help to her if he collapsed.

They had ridden for an hour. He had scanned the horizon for the past half hour, trying to see something beside cacti and scrub bushes. The sand dunes tricked him into thinking he saw buildings.

After an hour and a half he knew he had come far enough west. There was no sign of a mission. That meant it had to be either north or south of where they stood. Maybe they had come farther than twenty-five miles into the desert from the hills. That would mean they should now turn north. Or maybe they hadn't come far enough south.

He sat on his horse trying to decide. Then he awoke and realized his mind had been drifting. Was it for more than a few seconds? The heat was taking its toll.

Quickly he got off and checked Elizabeth. She had not changed. He rinsed her face again and emptied another canteen. They had only two more full canteens. That was just enough water to get them out of the desert. To stay for the rest of the day looking for the mission would not leave enough water to make it out.

He had to decide. They could turn north. If the mission weren't found, they could go on out of the desert. But she might not live as long as that would take. Or they could head south and, if no mission were found, then that would be the end of it.

He felt angry at having to make such a decision. With a violent jerk, he reined his horse toward the south. Maybe it was foolish. Maybe he was crazy from the heat. But he knew that if he had to find the mission, if it meant death for them both not to find it, then he would find it. Whenever everything was at stake, he did what had to be done. Maybe it was because his mind became more alert. Maybe it made him reach down within himself to come up with extra energy or courage or wisdom or something.

He didn't know why it was so, but he did know this one thing. Their best chance of winning was to bet everything on this one hand.

The horses plodded on.

He felt better now that the last decision was made. But the heat still was taking its toll. His mind was racing with daydreams and with thoughts about courage and bravery. Maybe that was part of survival, too. Maybe if he stopped and honestly considered their chances, he'd just stay right there and wait to die.

The horses stumbled more often now. They were exhausted. He got off and poured about a half canteen of water into his hat and watered them. Then he walked on foot for a few minutes and led them. He walked without thinking.

Suddenly he realized he was just standing, looking at the ground. And the horses were standing with their heads lowered. He shook his head, and he tried to clear his mind. He put his hand down on a prickly-pear leaf and pressed his palm into it until he flinched from the pain. That woke him enough to realize he must get into the saddle.

Back on the horse he saw a sand dune with a peculiar shape. He couldn't keep his eyes open. When he opened them next, the horses were still moving. He looked up to find the strange sand dune.

It was the mission. The bell tower of the brown adobe chapel rose above the dune.

He spoke quietly in a hoarse voice she couldn't hear, "Elizabeth, we've made it."

The mission was built like a fort. Tall adobe walls surrounded the chapel and several other buildings. The gates were open. The horses didn't need encouragement. They smelled the water inside and picked up their tired pace.

Five or six dark women were carrying water in buckets to rows of plants outside the walls. The children stopped their playing and stared at them as they rode in. One of the boys ran toward the chapel.

Seth rode along a row of low buildings lining the court-yard. He pulled up at the chapel and eased himself off the horse. Wearily he walked back to check on Elizabeth. He loosened the rawhide again on the nearly black leg. Her face still was burning and she made no movement or sound.

He tried to gather her in his arms to lift her, but he sank to one knee instead.

"Let me help you."

Seth looked up and saw a balding man in his middle forties in a coarse, brown robe. The man quickly examined her leg, then picked her up. With a rapid pace he walked around the chapel and through a doorway at the back. It was difficult for Seth to keep up.

When Seth entered the dark room, the man carrying Elizabeth was standing in a hallway calling to someone. A plump Mexican women emerged from the hallway wiping her hands on her dress. The man spoke to her rapidly and the women left. She came back in a few seconds with a candle.

She scurried to a wooden door in the floor near the corner of the room, lifted the door with a groan, and quickly descended a stairway holding the candle high. The man carrying Elizabeth followed.

Seth carefully held onto the railing as he shakily felt his way down the stairway. When he reached the earthen floor, Elizabeth already had been put on a narrow cot. The woman was loosening her clothes while the man was holding up the candle to look at the swollen leg.

The woman poured a bowl of water from an earthen jug. Then she poured water from her cupped hand onto

Elizabeth's burning face. The two talked in hushed voices as they worked.

The robed man then motioned for Seth to follow him upstairs. On the way up he said, "My name is Father Joseph. I hope we can save the woman. How long ago was she bitten?" The priest sat at a table, and Seth sank wearily into a chair across from him.

"The rattler bit her about eight hours ago. What are her chances, Padre?"

"We'll know soon. She would have died if you had not brought her here. She needed a cool place. That's why I took her to the cellar. If we can keep her temperature down, she'll stand a better chance.

"Consuela will bathe her with cool water and stay with her for now. I'll send one of the girls to get one of the Indian women to help her.

"We've had snake bites here before. The Papagos have been fairly successful in treating them by rubbing a liquid made from saguaro fruit on the wound and by giving the patient a special thick soup made from mescal and other desert plants. I'm not sure what's in it, but I've seen it work in several cases.

"These desert people have developed natural medicines over several hundred years. They rely on them. The woman is in the best hands you could find for hundreds of miles around."

Seth was grateful for the news. He closed his burning eyes. "Thank you for your help. I wasn't sure we'd make it."

"I'm sorry. You must be exhausted. Let me show you where you can wash the dust off and then I'll get some food brought to you. The boys will take care of your horses."

The cool well water soothed his burned face and the backs of his hands. It woke him up and made him realize how hungry he was. He hadn't eaten since breakfast.

A young Indian girl brought him bread and beans and fruit. As he ate, the priest told him that Mission San Miguel was built by Spanish Franciscans nearly two hundred years earlier to bring Christianity to the Indians. "The mission now is very quiet compared to its early years, when several priests and friars were here," he said. "Now I work with the Papagos and Mexicans, but I am the only priest. It's a fairly quiet place." He was lost in thought for a moment.

"Is the woman your wife?" he asked.

"No." Seth hesitated. "You might say I work for her."

The priest nodded and remained silent.

He seemed like a wise man to Seth. He would have to be dedicated to his work to live in a mission so far out in the desert.

"What brought you out here, Padre?"

Father Joseph stared out the window as he answered. "After many generations of Spanish missionaries, there were no replacements for those who died. So, since I was a young Franciscan priest in Boston who longed for more demanding work, I was sent out here to fill in for a year."

He smiled and folded his hands on the table. "That was sixteen years ago. The other friars are dead. I buried the last one four years ago."

"Padre, I admire your courage. This is rough country. Isn't it a difficult life?"

"Sometimes it is. Sometimes I remember the city and the changes of the seasons and the parties we had in school. And I miss sitting and talking to someone in English. That's why I'm glad to see you.

"But I've grown accustomed to this desert over the years. I tried to leave once and returned east. But before I got halfway back, I knew this had become my home. The Indians have taught me that this desert is not so desolate. They detect the subtle changes during the annual cycle. And the land is full of strange and wonderful forms of plants and animals, all struggling to survive.

"It may sound strange, but I find inspiration here. I can see life's great struggle going on all around me, and I feel that my own difficulties are just a regular part of the universe.

"I don't understand the Creator's plan and why it includes such struggle and suffering, but I do see life in a dramatic form here, and I can become one with it."

Father Joseph's words soothed Seth's worries about Elizabeth. He didn't understand what the priest was feeling exactly, but his words and the attitude in which he said them made Seth feel less anxious about her. Struggle and suffering were part of surviving, and Elizabeth was doing both. He wanted to check on her.

The plump woman moved aside when Seth came to the cot. Elizabeth seemed fitful. She was tossing her head and mumbling. He heard the word "Patty" and then it sounded like she was singing.

She moved quickly from a happy mood with a laugh to a frightened expression with faint cries of alarm. He heard her call his name and then call it again. Then she was quiet for a few minutes.

Seth felt helpless. All he could do was wait. He turned to the woman and wanted to thank her or talk with her. He could do neither. She smiled and said something in a musical tone. He smiled back and went upstairs.

He needed to sleep, but he would wait until he saw that Elizabeth was improving. The priest said they would know soon, after she had remained cool for a couple of hours.

He walked out of the priest's quarters into the warm evening air. He was surprised at how different the temperature was outside. The thick adobe walls made it much cooler inside than he had realized.

He began to walk. Low buildings with open doors and windows lined the entire courtyard. There was a well and a small garden on one side of the chapel. A few women scratched at the dust with hoes. A small man was herding five or six goats toward the gate. Other men and women were sitting in front of the low huts. Children played nearby.

On the other side of the chapel was a small orchard of fig trees. A cemetery held about a dozen grave markers. The door to the chapel was open. He entered and felt again the coolness the adobe walls provided. No one else was there.

He sat at the back on a rough plank bench. The walls were painted in bright colors, scenes from Bible stories, he supposed. Candles were burning in front at the altar. It seemed strange and mysterious to him. He had been in a church only twice in his life: once for the funeral of his grandfather and once when he got married.

He sat quietly. It felt good to sit in the cool silence. He thought about Elizabeth. If he were a praying man, he would pray for her recovery.

Although he wasn't a praying man, he did hope very much that she would live. That should count for something. He only knew the gods of the Greek stories he had read growing up. But he would feel silly praying to them. He always had just thought of them as characters in the stories.

Maybe it didn't matter if a man prayed to anyone or anything in particular. Maybe to sit and hope was a kind of prayer. Maybe caring about life was a sign to whatever gods there were that a man was paying tribute. If a Creator made life, then you paid a kind of tribute by caring about that creation.

He sat for a long while, thinking and hoping. Then he left and went back to the cellar to see Elizabeth. As he reached the bottom of the stairs the Mexican woman rose and smiled and gestured toward the cot.

Elizabeth's breathing was much easier now, not strained and rasping as before. Her color was more natural, and she wasn't tossing about. She seemed to be sleeping peacefully.

He was delighted. She was going to make it. No one had to tell him. He knew it. The woman seemed to know it, too. She patted Elizabeth's hand and nodded her own head vigorously.

He took Elizabeth's hand from the woman and held it for a moment. Elizabeth's soft skin was smooth against his calloused fingers. He carefully placed her hand back on the cot, watched her for a moment more, and then bounded up the stairs.

The evening was cooler now. He smiled broadly at the people he met crossing the courtyard. Father Joseph showed him to one of the low huts, where he spent the night.

Elizabeth was awake when Seth entered the cellar the next morning. She spoke sleepily, "So you didn't leave me out there after all, Seth." Her smile was a wonderful sight to him.

"I had to bring you along, Elizabeth. There's no one else who can tell campfire stories like you." They talked for a few minutes. She was very weak, but she was able to take some of the broth the woman fed her. She drifted off to sleep again after a few spoonsful.

Seth spent the day helping the men with the goats and a small, scrawny herd of cattle kept outside the mission wall. He also helped the women water the fruit trees and the vegetable garden. They giggled at him, thinking it was strange he was doing that work.

He laughed when they laughed. He was happy to be working, to be alive, and to be planning to travel on with Elizabeth soon.

By early afternoon Elizabeth was awake again and they moved her to one of the adobe huts. Her leg already was back to its normal size, but she still was weak.

Father Joseph looked at her leg and shook his head. "I don't understand it. Papago medicine in Consuela's hands does remarkable things. You folks came to the right place."

The next day Elizabeth could limp about the courtyard for short periods and watch the children play. In two more days she was restless to travel. They had more than a full day's ride across the desert back to Sandstone Creek. So they decided that the next day they would leave in the late afternoon after the hottest part of the day and be within one day's ride of Sandstone Creek when they stopped and camped.

As they rode out the mission gateway, Seth turned and saw Father Joseph standing in the courtyard watching them leave. He looked like a man who was very much at home.

At dusk they made camp out in the open as before, so it would not appear that they were hiding. Elizabeth hadn't complained about her leg during the ride, but she began limping more noticeably as they prepared camp. Without a doubt, she had become much tougher since he first saw her in that buckboard peering out at him from under that fashionable straw hat.

They talked about the mission and Father Joseph before turning in. The desert no longer looked as hostile now. They knew that it contained an oasis, and they knew they could survive.

CHAPTER 12

SOMETHING was wrong, and Seth sensed it even before he opened his eyes. The muffled thud of a horse's hoof, the swish of a tail, the movement of a shadow across his face.

They were circled by seven or eight men. He knew they had to be Papagos. He glanced over at Elizabeth. He was glad she still was asleep.

He sat up slowly. A couple of them had rifles pointed at him. He raised his hands above the blankets to show that his hands were empty.

The Indians seemed to be in no hurry. He had no idea how long they had been standing there.

"Elizabeth," Seth spoke with a husky, dry voice. "Elizabeth, we've got company."

She rolled over and looked at him, then sat up quickly, wide-eyed. "Take it easy. Just be still."

He stood slowly and waited. He would show no fear and would not deceive them about anything. Most of them wore leather or cotton pants and either loose-fitting shirts or vests. One of the men brought their horses over and gestured for them to mount.

They rode at an easy pace for about an hour. Seth saw that Elizabeth was frightened but was trying not to show it. Riding seemed to be painful for her still. She needed another day or two to recover.

They came to a village of cattle-hide tepees at the edge of a ravine. Small cottonwoods meant a spring at the bottom.

The village women and children stared at them as they
rode into the loose cluster of shelters. He and Elizabeth dismounted when the others did. Their horses were lead away.
One of the men disappeared into a tepee near the center of
the village and reappeared with another man, about Seth's
age. The man was shorter than the others, had black hair to
his shoulders, and walked with a slight limp.

"You've been brought here because we want to ask you
some questions." His smooth English brought a surprised
look to Seth's face. The man saw his surprise but offered no
explanation.

"You are either brave or foolish for coming into our
desert. The white is not wanted here. We do not live easily
with the white man as a neighbor in the valley. But now you
must answer some questions."

The man led them into the dark tepee and told them to sit
down. Seth could make out the figure of a man before them
with long gray hair. As his eyes adjusted to the dark, Seth
saw that the man had an extremely wrinkled face. The old
man sat motionless, dressed in buckskin trousers. He had a
robe made of animal skin around his shoulders.

The old man spoke to them looking directly at them, first
one and then the other. The language was different from
any Seth had heard. It didn't have the harshness of Apache,
and the man spoke it slowly and softly.

Their guide then spoke English. "Chief Akimoel wants to
know about the horse the woman is riding. Where did you
get it and where have you come from on it?"

Seth was startled. Surely they didn't think the horse was
stolen from them. He thought back quickly. Elizabeth was
riding the buckskin that he had brought at Jake's the day of
the hearing.

He wasn't sure what the right answer would be, what answer they wanted to hear, but he remembered what the
prospector had said. His best chance was to tell the truth.
They'd probably know if he didn't.

"I bought the horse eight days ago." He looked at the interpreter first, then at the chief. "I bought it in Black Springs from a blacksmith named Jake."

The old man heard the translation, nodded once, and spoke again.

"Did you speak with the man who shoes horses who is called Jake?"

"He did not speak to me in words," Seth answered. "But he spoke to me like this." He made the gesture with the fist and the open palm.

The old man did not wait for the translation but spoke to the interpreter at a faster pace.

"He wants to know what you did to receive this sign."

"I don't know for sure, because I don't know what the sign means. But before Jake made the sign, I killed a man who wanted to kill him."

The next question came quickly. "Were you a friend of this man called Jake?"

"I traded with him and did business with him, but I did not know him well. Since then he has helped me and I would be his friend if I lived in Black Springs."

"If you were not then his friend, why did you kill the man who wanted to kill him?"

Seth thought back to the shooting. "The man who wanted to kill him had no good reason to kill him, and Jake did not carry a weapon."

The chief listened and then remained silent. Seth said, "May I ask a question?"

The interpreter nodded, and Seth asked him, "Why do you ask about the horse? Have you seen it before?"

The interpreter delivered the question, and the chief muttered a word or two. The interpreter answered.

"That horse has been shod in the past few days. The shoes bear a special mark. There is a small dent on the side of each shoe that leaves in the earth the mark of a rising sun. Every Papago craftsman leaves his own mark on his work to show that it is his. He takes pride in his work, whatever it is. The man you call Jake is a Papago, and the rising sun is his mark."

The interpreter stopped talking, and the chief remained silent. Seth saw that they were through. But he wasn't sure what would happen to Elizabeth and him now. She wasn't ready for more hard desert travel just yet.

"I would like to ask another question," Seth said.

The interpreter nodded.

"We would like permission to stay in your land and rest for two or three days. I should tell you that we are running from the law and it could mean trouble for you."

The chief's expression did not change as he heard the translation. "Akimoel wants to know what you did to make the lawmen chase you."

"The woman with me took money that had been taken from her by a wealthy man."

The chief looked at Elizabeth as he answered.

"He says that you may stay. The Papagos know that it is not wrong to run from the white man's law if you have done no wrong. We know what it is to take back what has been taken from you. You may stay in our land and you may stay with us in this village, where there is water.

The chief muttered two or three words, and the interpreter stood and gestured for them to go.

Outside the tepee, the interpreter extended his hand. "My name is Pimawa. I know English because I have worked on some ranches in the valley. Akimoel is our religious leader and teacher. We call him the Keeper of the Smoke. In your language he would be called a chief.

"Akimoel did not show it with his face, but he is pleased with the news of the man you call Jake. The man is Akimoel's only son, and his Papago name is Tahmawo."

They were surprised to hear that news. "I thought Jake was an unusual man," Elizabeth said. "He helped me make a good trade when I bought two horses at his shop."

Pimawa laughed. "That sounds like Tahmawo. I've known him since he was born. He always has loved horses and knows them well."

"Why isn't he living here with his people?" Seth asked.

Pimawa told them the story as he walked with them to the village's edge, where they were to camp. "When Tahmawo was about twelve years old some cattle from a valley ranch wandered into our own herd. The white ranchers found them and thought we had stolen the cattle. They wanted to teach our people a lesson. But the white man did not know where we were camped.

"We move our village with the seasons. In those days we wintered in the Baboquivari Mountains to the east, where water is plentiful.

"Tahmawo was out learning to hunt alone, as boys do when they reach their twelfth year. The ranchers found him and made him tell where the people were camped. They must have hurt him very much to make him tell.

"The ranchers then rode up to our camp and began shooting the horses and livestock. Some of them also shot into the tepees to frighten us. Tahmawo's mother and his baby sister were in one of the tepees. They were killed. Chief Akimoel's heart was broken by the death of his wife and daughter, and he banished Tahmawo from the tribe for telling where to find the camp.

"Tahmawo swore then that he never would speak again as long as he lived outside the tribe. He also suffered much inside himself because of what happened.

"For a few years he worked on a ranch in Mexico, where he learned the work of a blacksmith. He was good at that work. Ranchers began bringing work to him. Then he opened the shop in Black Springs and has been there for many years.

"The killing was about fourteen years ago. Father and son have not spoken since. But Akimoel always wants to hear news of his son. That's why he asked about the horse.

He loves Tahmawo, but he is a proud chief. Tahmawo is a proud man, too. The old man may die without seeing his son again."

Seth and Elizabeth spent two days in the Papago village. They talked about Pimawa's story of Jake and the old chief. They also watched the children at play and sampled the women's corn cakes and the saguaro cactus candy. They heard more stories from Pimawa and tried the strong, clear drink he called "agave," which was made from mescal and tasted like raw whiskey.

The people still watched them with curiosity, but there seemed to be little hostility except from some of the older people. They must have remembered how it was before the white man came to the valley.

On the morning of the third day, Seth and Elizabeth broke camp and got ready to go. It had been nearly two weeks since Elizabeth had walked out of Tucson Cattlemen's Bank. That day seemed like months before to both of them.

Seth had been thinking about Jake and the old chief during their stay in the village. It was a problem familiar to him. He didn't want to leave without talking to the chief again.

Akimoel walked about the village once in the morning and once in the afternoon. The rest of the time he remained in his tepee, and his people consulted him there.

Seth asked Pimawa if he could speak with Akimoel before they left. Pimawa returned a few minutes later and led them to the tepee.

When they were seated, Seth looked into the tired old eyes and spoke softly. "You and your people have been kind to us. Right now I can return that kindness only with words. I would like to speak to the chief of the Papagos about his son Tahmawo, the man we call Jake."

He waited for some response. The chief was silent, then nodded just slightly. Seth wasn't sure if that was permission to speak. Pimawa nodded to go ahead.

"My bond with Tahmawo gives me the strength to speak boldly. You have seen many hot summers in this desert, Akimoel, and that has given you much wisdom. But there is something I have learned that the chief of the Papagos has not."

Pimawa hesitated, looked at Seth for a moment, and then translated to the chief. Seth knew there was a risk the old man might become angry.

He continued, "I have learned that if a man does not spit out the bitter water of yesterday, he cannot taste the sweet water of tomorrow. I have learned that today is like a stream that we cross. We leave the land of the past and enter the land of the future. If we cross that stream walking backward so we see only the land we leave, we may lose the trail as we enter a new land."

Seth knew he must not stop now or he might not get to finish. The chief probably knew what was coming next.

"Akimoel, I am speaking of your son, Tahmawo. He is a brave and a good man. He does not speak, yet he always tells the truth. The truth he tells with his life and his work and his courage is that he is the son of a chief. His life also tells that he is a man with a great love. Deep within him is a love for his people and for his father.

"Don't ask how I know this, for I cannot tell you. But I know it. I have talked with Tahmawo in the way that men talk in silence.

"I also know this, Akimoel. There is pain in the heart of the chief of the Papagos because he longs for his son. And I have seen that same pain in Tahmawo, who longs for his father. I did not know what caused Tahmawo that pain until I sat in this tepee.

"The Papagos will need Tahmawo one day when you are not here to lead them. And Tahmawo needs to be among his people again.

"I am a stranger among the Papagos, and a guest in the tepee of their chief. I have no place to speak these words.

But I speak them as a bond brother of Tahmawo, and I speak them as one who has suffered the hurt of yesterday also.

"If I cause pain, Akimoel, it is the pain given by one who tries to heal. It is the cut of the knife that lets the snake poison flow out. I speak as one who is still healing from that kind of snake bite."

He stopped talking now. He had said all he could. He felt drained. He had not been aware that he felt all these things and he didn't know he could say them to someone else. But he knew the old man's pain. And he knew the value of what he told him.

Akimoel sat still, his eyes closed. After a few minutes, Pimawa gestured that they should leave. Outside the tepee Seth and Elizabeth walked to their horses in silence. As they started to ride off, Pimawa stopped them.

"Seth March, thank you for what you have done today. The chief heard what many of us have wanted to tell him for many years. We could not because he is our chief. But he listened to you because you were his guest and because you spoke bravely."

"What do you think will happen now?" Seth asked.

"Now that Akimoel has heard, he will think in silence. His silence means that he knows the truth of your words and is wrestling with them. He is a good chief, Seth, and a wise one. But he also is a father and he loved the mother of his son. I think others in the tribe can talk with him now about Tahmawo. I think Tahmawo may be with us again soon. Thank you for that."

They began their long day's trek across the desert basin, riding again through an endless world of cacti and mesquite and creosote bushes. He could not speak to Elizabeth just yet. But he soon he would be ready to tell her the rest of his story.

CHAPTER 13

ELIZABETH was becoming accustomed to the long rides now and even enjoyed the quietness of the desert and the mind-clearing monotony of the plodding horses.

They rode all day beneath the blazing sun out of the desert basin and northeast into Santa Cruz Valley. They were headed toward Sandstone Creek and the money.

At dusk they stopped and ate supper, watered the horses, and rested. They decided to wait until dark to ride the last few miles. Seth had hidden the money in an open area. In the daylight they could easily be seen if anyone happened to be around.

As they waited in the gathering dusk, they talked about their plans after getting the money. She felt sad now that the journey was almost over. After tonight their reason for being together would end.

She told him she wanted to see if the girls had gone on to San Francisco. If they had, she would follow.

Seth told her of his plans to head west to California. Now he was able to tell her more about Louise and of his overwhelming grief during three years of wandering after her death. He told her that he had to visit Louise's grave and finally bury her in his mind. He would try to begin again with his ranch in San Joaquin Valley.

She was moved by his story. It explained what had been troubling him. It also meant that he had been especially kind in stopping to help her for these two weeks, even risking his life. But she wondered if he might have been doing it only because she reminded him of Louise.

It didn't matter. He had saved her life. Also, he finally had told her his story. She was grateful for that, too.

It was dark when they slowly began the final leg of their journey. They headed back to where it all began for them. Across the valley, over a rise, and about two hours later they were looking down on Sandstone Creek.

They reined in and quietly surveyed the scene. Seth seemed worried about it. There was an old shack about halfway down the slope to the creek. They waited for several minutes before descending and then made a wide circle around the shack, just in case.

They stopped again and waited and listened. There was only the distant muffled gurgling of the creek. No movement. No other sounds.

Finally Seth motioned to her and they rode into the campsite. The moon was full and the sky was cloudless. They dismounted and tied the horses. Seth's mare seemed skittish.

"I don't like it, Liz," Seth said softly. She was nervous and barely noticed that he had just called her "Liz" for the first time. "It's too quiet." He listened for a moment more.

"Maybe it's just my imagination." He smiled and spoke louder. "I'm pretty sure we weren't followed, and it's been over a week since the jailbreak. They've probably forgotten about us by now."

She suspected he was just trying to ease her nervousness. "I know what you mean," she said. "We've been chased and watched and surprised for so many days now, it's beginning to work on me, too. Let's get the money and go."

Seth decided not to tell her yet that the money was hidden in the cottonwood tree down the creek. In case they had an audience for this last act everything had to go the way he had planned it.

He glanced around once more, then paced off twenty

steps up the hill from the campsite and stopped. The area was clear of trees and brush. He looked about on the ground, found the patch of fresh earth, and began digging with his knife and hands. She watched while he scooped handsful of loose dirt out of the hole.

"There it is!" She said it louder than she intended.

The top of a white sack with a red ribbon poked up through the loose dirt in the bottom of the hole. He leaned down to uncover the rest.

A twig snapped behind them. They both turned quickly.

"That's right, folks. I'm right behind you." A tall man holding a pistol stood just out of the shadows. He was grinning. She knew immediately who it was. This was the man the prospector had described.

"Hello, Kirby," Seth said. "I figured you wouldn't give up easily. Been waiting long?"

"I can be a patient man, March, when it comes to settlin' a score. I knew you'd be back sooner or later. This had to be the only place the money could be stashed."

He paused, feeling the satisfaction of being right. "And now it's mine. And so are you." He grinned at her. "Both of you."

Kirby took Seth's pistol and flung it away. "Now keep diggin' and let's have that sack."

Seth removed more dirt and began to tug on the sack. "I can't believe you were smart enough to figure it out, Kirby. I think you must have had help." Seth kept digging.

Elizabeth knew Seth must be trying to provoke him. But she was frightened at the thought of what Kirby might do if he got angry.

"I knew you had the money, March. But you're right, I had a little help." His laugh ended with a sneer. "And it will be a pleasure to tell you how I got the help." He turned to her. "Let's just say I persuaded one of your lady friends to tell me that you dropped off the money here on your way by."

She gasped and stepped toward him.

"Easy, little lady. I didn't hurt her much. I just helped her remember." He grinned again.

"Who was it?" she demanded. She hated to think of one of the girls hurt because of her.

"Well, ma'am, I'd love to tell you, but we wasn't formally introduced, so I didn't make her acquaintance. I did get a real good look at her, though. She was the young, blond one. I figured she would remember a little faster than the others."

Elizabeth felt sick. She tried not to show her fear. She wanted to run or to cry. She knew neither would help. She would have to trust Seth to do something.

Seth pulled the sack out of the hole and pitched it down in front of Kirby. "There it is. Now take it and leave us alone."

"Oh, you'd like that, wouldn't you, March. Just buy me off with the money. Well, that's not enough anymore, cowpuncher. You owe me much more than that. And I've been waitin' here day and night to collect." Kirby picked up the sack with his left hand and tested its weight. He still held the pistol in his right.

"I want to thank you for bringin' along your lady friend. That's goin' to make my collectin' a lot more fun." He laughed cynically. "I figure you've grown real fond of her by now. And you wouldn't want to see anythin' happen to her, would you?"

He pitched the sack back at Seth. "Just bring that along. We're goin' for a short hike."

They walked ahead of Kirby the half mile up the slope to the shack they had seen earlier. They entered and heard a rat scurrying across the floor.

Kirby seemed to know his way around inside. He headed straight for a table and fumbled with something. The room brightened as he lit a kerosene lamp. He ordered them to sit down.

The room contained only a rickety table and two chairs.

A shelf above the fireplace held a few dishes. An open doorway led to another room at the back.

She and Seth sat in the two chairs. She looked at Seth. His face was expressionless. She couldn't detect any signs of fear. There was only determination in his eyes. She wondered how he would handle the situation if she weren't there. Her presence limited his options.

For the first time she realized what risks she had been asking him to take just because of the money. It seemed almost funny to her that now, in this situation where their chances of survival were slim, she realized she loved him.

Suddenly she heard the dry, cold click of the gun being cocked. It chilled her whole body. The pistol was pointed at Seth.

"I'll have them put it on your grave marker, March: 'His one big mistake was kickin' a man while he was down.'"

Seth spoke calmly. "I think you're right, Kirby. I shouldn't have kicked you in the head back there in Chelsey's. I should have let you go for your gun."

Seth leaned back in the chair and smiled. "At least I'll die happy, Kirby, knowing you'll be hanged for murder. Everybody will figure that a man who beats up young girls wouldn't have the guts to face me in a fair gunfight."

The gun flashed fire and Seth crashed to the floor. Elizabeth screamed. He thrased about, holding his leg. Through clenched teeth he swore at Kirby.

Kirby was enjoying it. "I was going to let you die like a man, March, real quick-like. But now I want to see you squirm."

The gun roared again. This time Seth clutched his left arm and moaned softly. He glared at Kirby defiantly.

She could stand it no more. "Stop it! Please stop! Please don't shoot him again!" She was crying and knelt down beside Seth. She could see the dark stain spreading under his fingers where he was holding his arm.

Seth said to her in a low, hoarse voice, "Get away, Liz.

Get out of here when he shoots again. Just run. It's your only chance."

"No!" she shouted, crying. "No! You can't do this!" She stood up and faced Kirby. "What do you want?" The tears were streaming down her face, but anger had replaced her fear.

"I'll give you whatever you want if you'll just stop shooting him." She spoke coldly, with hate in her voice. "Do you want me? Is that what you want?"

Kirby smiled. "March, seems like you met a real loyal woman here. And a real hellcat, too. That's good. I like 'em feisty." Kirby leered at her. "Why don't you and me go see what kind of a deal we can work out."

Kirby lifted the lamp higher and gestured toward the back room. She swallowed hard and tried not to think about what was coming. It all seemed like a dream. It wasn't really happening. She moved toward the doorway, where Kirby was waiting.

"No, Elizabeth," Seth said, pleading.

"I guess we've heard about enough from you, March." Kirby lifted the pistol and aimed. A shot rang out. Kirby spun around and crashed into the wall. The lamp shattered on the wooden floor, and the fire quickly spread in a widening circle.

"Seth!" she screamed and began tugging him toward the front door. The heat already was intense as the fire climbed the wall. His trousers were on fire. She pulled harder, trying to drag him out.

Suddenly somebody was beside her, helping her pull Seth, and then the cool, fresh air surrounded them. They were out.

She began slapping at the fire on Seth's pants. Then gloved hands were there, too, smothering the flames. She looked up. It was Marshal Brenner.

She remembered the money. "Seth, the money's still in

there!" She stood and tried to run back toward the shack, but Seth was holding her tightly around the ankle.

"No, Liz. Don't go back in there." He held on firmly, even when she gave up trying to run. He tried to speak, to tell her something, then he passed out.

The cabin was engulfed in flames now. She helped Brenner drag Seth farther away from the scorching heat, then collapsed on the ground beside him.

She knew the money was gone, but they were still alive. She watched the roof crash into the inferno, throwing bright sparks high into the clear night sky.

CHAPTER 14

SETH March awoke in a blur of whiteness. His eyes focused on a whitewashed ceiling and walls in a room that was neat and simply furnished. Curtains were blowing gently at the window. Shafts of sunlight brightened the floor.

Elizabeth dozed in a rocking chair beside the bed. He tried to roll in her direction and felt the aches and stiffness in his leg and arm. He became aware of the pain. He also felt weak and hungry.

"Liz," he said softly. Quickly she awoke. She smiled and sat on the bed beside him.

"Welcome back, Seth. You've been sleeping for almost a whole day."

"What happened after I blacked out? I saw Brenner there."

"He helped me bring you here. We're at a homesteader's farm about two miles east of the creek. We didn't think we should take you all the way into Black Springs. You were bleeding too much. The Ramseys patched you up until Doc McKinney got here."

"The Ramseys?"

"Jason and Rachael Ramsey. This is their place. They're Quakers. They're opposed to guns and violence, but they're willing to help people in trouble, even people with gunshot wounds."

Mrs. Ramsey was a short, plump woman who always seemed to be wearing a clean, starched apron over a gray dress. She had a round face with rosy cheeks and kept her brown hair in a bun at the back of her head. When she came in now and then to check on him, two boys about four and six years old stared from the doorway. Late in the afternoon, she came in and announced that he had a visitor.

Brenner entered awkwardly. He seemed ill at ease in this clean, neat house. He was glad Seth was well enough to talk.

"How ya doin', Seth?" He pulled a chair up to the bed.

"Well enough, Marshal. But not in any position to give you any more trouble. We're both alive and we're obliged to you for that. Let us know when you want us in Black Springs and we'll be there."

"That's one of the things I need to talk with you about. I wired that Tucson bank this morning and told them the money was burned up. I said that I would have arrested their employee, Roscoe Kirby, for attempted murder except that he got burned up, too.

"I then asked them about your story, Miss Castle, about their refusing to give you your money even though the court said it was yours.

"They wired back that they wanted to drop the charges and asked me to close the case. I figure they lost interest when they heard about the money. They're probably also nervous about not obeying the court. I aim to ask the marshal in Tucson to check into that."

Seth was relieved to hear the news. There still was the matter of the jail escape. "Where does that leave us now, Marshal? Elizabeth escaped from the jail and I helped her. I pretended to be a deputy. . . ."

"And I lied a little at the hearing," Elizabeth said. "What are those offenses going to cost us?"

Brenner exploded. "Damn your hide, March. How could you trick me like that, smuggling that derringer in right under my nose? And me with a busted arm?" His eyes glared out of his broad, wrinkled face.

He turned to Elizabeth. "Is he well enough for me to scold?"

Without waiting for an answer, he continued. "I ought to make you wear that deputy badge you stole and make you work for me in Black Springs for a year or two. That'd be a punishment fittin' the crime." The glare had turned to a twinkle, and he pulled at his drooping, white moustache.

"And as for you, young lady, that was about the most far-fetched, bold-faced story I've ever heard in all my days in this law business. And those blame fools I try to protect believed it." He chuckled. "If I hadn't been so busy trying to keep them from busting each other's heads, I would have enjoyed that brawl."

Brenner was more serious now. "It's against the law to bust out of jail. But as I see it, ma'am, you had no cause to be charged with bank robbery in the first place. And since nobody got hurt when you busted out . . . well . . . I'm willing to forget about it."

Brenner chuckled again. "Of course, there's Tommy Myers. He won't forget it anytime soon. He was pretty embarrassed about your taking his clothes and leaving him tied up. But he needed some of the starch taken out of him."

"Marshal, Kirby told us he made one of my girls tell him about the money. What did he do to her?"

"Kirby slapped her about and she got bruised up some. Mostly he just scared her. She came and told me about it afterward 'cause she was afraid of what might happen to you two if he caught up with you.

"That's how I knew to go out there," he continued. "I figured he'd be waiting for you. I got out there after you'd already gone up to that shack. Then I heard the first shot.

With my busted arm still in a sling, I figured I'd have only one chance to shoot him. So I crawled up right to the window. I didn't get there until he had already put a couple of slugs in you."

He pulled on his moustache again. "Sorry about being a little late, Seth. But Doc McKinney hasn't had much to do lately. I thought he'd appreciate getting the work."

Seth laughed and winced from the pain. "Thanks for getting there when you did. I thought if I could get Kirby riled up a bit, he'd make a mistake. I figure his wanting to watch me die slowly probably saved my life and cost him his. Thanks for making it work out that way."

Brenner stood up and walked to the door. "Forget it, Seth. I suppose we're even. And Doc McKinney now has a total of three slugs for his lead statue."

He opened the door. "By the way, some Papagos came into town this morning and talked with Jake. I think he might be going back to his people. Sure hate to lose a good blacksmith.

"Oh, and I have a message for you, Miss Castle. Those other four women, they decided to keep that appointment in San Francisco. They said if I saw you again to let you know they had gone on out. You got a loyal bunch of friends there. They knew you were trying to clear them when you left them behind in the jail. I let them go after you two cleared out of town.

"One last thing, folks. As soon as you can travel, will you get out of this territory? You've caused me about all the trouble I can stand for a long while." He looked at Elizabeth for a moment, then back at Seth.

"Here's some good advice, Seth. Take this woman with you wherever you're going next and marry her. The territory won't be a safe place for anybody as long as she's running loose." With a hoarse laugh and then a fit of coughing, Brenner was gone.

Seth looked at her. She was blushing. "You know, Liz, the marshal is right. You are a dangerous woman." He changed the subject to save them both embarrassment.

"We're free people again. No reward for our capture. No posse to chase us . . ."

"And no money," she said. "I guess I'll go to San Francisco, join the girls, and start all over again."

It seemed to him Elizabeth really didn't care that much about the money. Maybe she felt as he did, that it'd be tough to go their separate ways now. They had been traveling together for only a week or so, but they had faced ten years' worth of life and death. Now that it was over, there wasn't the relief they both had expected.

But there was one more step to take in their journey.

The next day he felt well enough to get out of bed. The day after that he suggested a short ride. They borrowed a wagon from Mr. Ramsey. The friendly, black-bearded farmer hitched the team for them. He helped Seth climb up to the seat and handed Elizabeth the reins. Then he stood back with his belly bulging over his belt and sent them off with a hearty, "Godspeed!"

Seth asked Elizabeth to drive back to Sandstone Creek and the campsite. He explained, "It's for old times' sake, Liz."

At the campsite, she tied the reins to the seat and they climbed down. "I want to show you something interesting," he said and took her to a cottonwood tree near the creek. The tree had a hollow in it about four feet from the ground hidden by a sumac bush.

"Put your hand in there, Liz."

"No," she said, laughing. "You're crazy. There probably are squirrels in that hole."

He grinned broadly. "Trust me."

"Okay, I'll be foolish just once more. Here goes." She closed her eyes and thrust her hand into the hole. Nothing happened at first. Then she cautiously began to feel around. Suddenly her face lit up in surprise.

"Seth, it can't be!" she shouted. In disbelief she pulled out a bundle of bills with a wrapper reading, "Tucson Cattlemen's Bank."

She began laughing and raking out bundle after bundle. The pile at her feet grew until the tree hollow was empty. She sat down on the pile of money and looked at him accusingly.

"Okay, Seth March, let's have it. You haven't been honest with me."

He confessed that he had stuffed the flour sack with prairie grass and leaves and had added a few rocks for weight He had buried it instead of the money in case someone like Kirby might be waiting for them to return.

"That was why I stopped you from going back into the burning shack after the money. I knew the money wasn't in there."

"If I weren't so happy, I'd be angry with you for not telling me."

"What are you going to do with the money now?" he asked.

"I'm not sure what I'll do with my share. I doubt I'll put it in a bank again. Some of it goes to the girls in San Francisco, and some of it is yours. I promised you a share, and you've certainly earned it."

She looked at him for a moment. "Those are all the plans I have for now."

He searched those piercing eyes for a clue to what was on her mind. Then he cleared his throat and began. "Elizabeth Castle, how would you like to take on an old partner in a new venture? This time it'll be my land in California and your money, and we both can go out there and start a cattle ranch."

She wrapped her arms around his neck. He flinched from

the pain in his arm. She quickly backed off and then kissed him gently.

"Seth March, I guess I've been wanting that kind of partner for some time. Maybe that's why I took your horse when we first met here. Maybe I wanted to see you again."

He looked skeptically at her. "Could be. But more likely, you took my horse because you didn't know yours had only picked up a stone."

"Was that all? Why didn't you tell me then?"

"Maybe I wanted to see you again," he said.

CHAPTER 15

SETH March stepped back and read once more the grave marker he had just pounded in place.

"Louise March, 1862–1882"

He looked at her grave, covered with grass. It was on a knoll which flowed like a sea of green down to the valley floor and to the San Joaquin River. He stood alone. This was a private farewell.

Again he spoke softly the lines that had been so important to him from the story about Orpheus: *"The bud was plucked before the flower bloomed. I tried to bear my loss. I could not bear it. Love was too strong a god."*

But he knew he could bear it now. Not because he loved the memory of Louise any less, but because he realized the truth in the rest of Orpheus' words. He opened a book and read:

O gods who rule the dark and silent world,
You are the debtor who is always paid.
A little while we tarry up on earth.
Then we are yours forever and forever.

Seth continued to speak softly. "This is what I needed most, Louise, to say good-bye, to bury the dead. I want to remember the past with gratitude for the good things, but I must try not to cling to it."

He took a final look at the grave and the marker. Memories began to flood his mind: her face, her laugh, the sight of her strolling across this land.

He took a deep breath and tried to swallow away the ache in his throat. He turned and began walking down the gentle slope. His land spread out before him, rich earth and green grass, and a stand of birch above the valley floor where the shack now stood and where the ranch house would be built soon.

Then his gaze moved to the bottom of the slope, where Elizabeth sat in the buckboard.

All of this gave him life. It was Louise and this land that had brought him back, and it was Elizabeth who would help him build a future.

Suddenly Seth stopped. He clenched his fist and touched his chest once and then moved his open hand up toward the knoll where Louise was buried and down toward Elizabeth waiting for him, and finally out toward the sea of grass and the river and the blue sky which stretched forever.